*The story of Gary Paine
as told to his friend, the teacher*

Nachzehrer

Nelson Keane

GALLEON

First Galleon Edition, June 2024
ISBN 978-1-998122-09-7

Published by Galleon Books
Moncton, New Brunswick, Canada
www.galleonbooks.ca

Cover artwork © Jacob Blanchet.
pictishdreams@gmail.com

Nachzehrer, a novel, is a true story, every word of it, or else it wouldn't exist. And if within these pages you find any resemblence to ghouls in your life, present or past or future, then you, as well, are a true story.

Library and Archives Canada Cataloguing in Publication

Title: Nachzehrer / Nelson Keane.
Names: Keane, Nelson, author.
Identifiers: Canadiana 20240382927 | ISBN 9781998122097 (softcover)
Subjects: LCGFT: Novels.
Classification: LCC PS8621.E22 N33 2024 | DDC C813/.6—dc23

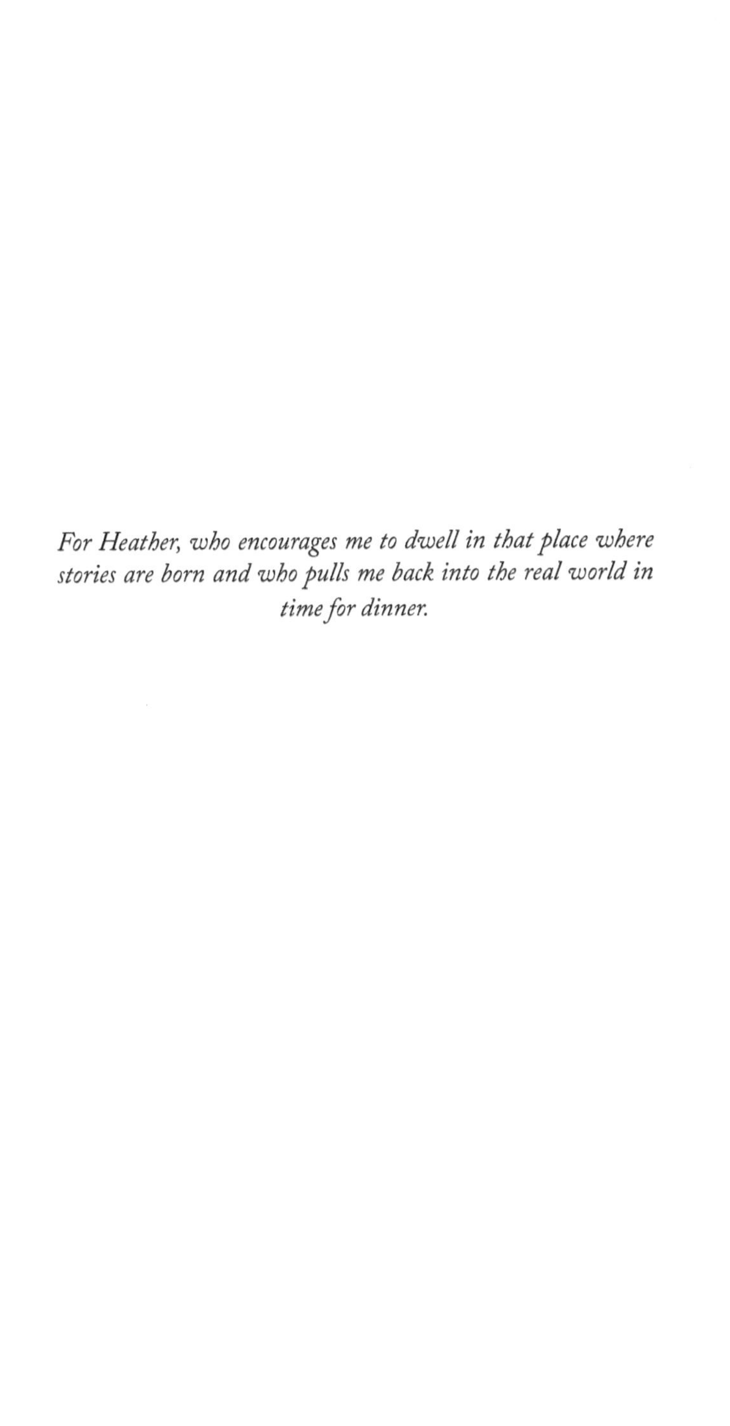

For Heather, who encourages me to dwell in that place where stories are born and who pulls me back into the real world in time for dinner.

Obituary

There was an obituary in the newspaper last week, a man I had known for forty years. He was ninety-nine years old and died because he was tired and because his X-ray goggles would not work. I say that I knew him for forty years, but while that is true, it is also a lie. I knew him for fifteen minutes every day, Monday to Friday. But, alas, those fifteen minutes added up, I suppose.

I know his obituary by heart, because I wrote it.

Gerald Kurt Paine (Gary to his friends), one of the last great generation of heroes, December 21, 1918 – November 7, 2018. Gerald Paine — Flying Officer in the Royal Air Force; Battle of Britain pilot in his thunderous Hurricane with its V-12 engine; prisoner of war; tortured and forgotten man — loved to listen to the cold rain splatter on the plastic sheet that covered the cardboard box he called home. He died playing the violin and remembering his American. Gerald's body was ninety-nine years old, but his soul had been eaten when he was twenty-five years young.

Services will be held under the overpass across from the Walmart on King Street, at five minutes to five p.m. on November 11. There will be no eulogy, but all present will be asked to think about those who have suffered and remember that Gary loved truth above all else. Please pause for a moment and listen to his friend play a song on the violin that had special meaning for our departed *diekhaulder*. Please take a five-dollar bill from the blue recycling box before you leave.

Chaos and Chance

I met Gerald Kurt Paine when I was driving to my first and, as it turned out, only adult job. It was September 1978, and my teaching degree, newly inked, was hanging on a wall in my parents' house. I was about to do something that would alter my life forever. The gods of chaos must have been crowded into the back seat of my car that day, laughing and crying.

I was twenty-two years old and driving a red 1978 Ford Mustang convertible that I had convinced a bank to let me buy. The top was down and the song on the radio was asking who I was as I sped down the off-ramp from the highway. I stopped at a red light and glanced to my right. Staring down into the car was the handsomest man I imagined could ever exist on this planet. He reminded me of the actor Paul Newman in *Cool Hand Luke*, but even more like Newman than the original. His piercing blue eyes had a twinkle in them. I would never have known he was a homeless panhandler, but for the World War II Royal Air Force pilot's uniform he wore and the heavy steel German military helmet that covered his head. To top it off he had flying goggles hanging around his neck, like antique jewellery.

He laughed as he considered my new car and said, "Let me guess, young man. New car, new job, and twenty-two. Am I correct?"

I said, "Yes. Is it that obvious?"

He did not answer my question. Instead he leaned on the door of my car and said, "When I was twenty-two, my first real adult job was on August 13, 1940. Do you know what happened that day? Besides my first day of real work, when I was twenty-two, just like you."

I was nervous. "Is that when the war started? My dad was in it, you know. He was in the infantry — a corporal with the Canadian Army at Juno Beach."

"Good about your dad, but not so good about knowing the date I gave you. Well, young man driving a nice red car on the way to his first job — teaching, I suppose — try again," he said.

The light had turned green by then, but because I was early for work and I had to know about that date and why he had asked the question of me, a stranger, I parked my car near the corner and returned to the man who seemed to know me so well.

"Ah, intrigued are you, young teacher with very large car payments?" he said as I approached on foot, my longish hair flapping in synch with my stupid wide paisley tie.

I smiled and said, "This may not mean that much to you, but I'll be teaching history this year. I like your hat and your protective eyewear, but it looks like a heavy load to carry around with you all day."

The man laughed, tapped the heavy steel with his knuckles, and replied, "The uniform is mine, well-earned and impossible to discard. The helmet was given to me as a gift a long time ago, in a terrible place where monsters lived and where souls were eaten. Those soul-eaters and monsters are still searching for me, and these goggles help me see them coming. The helmet serves a different purpose."

He adjusted the goggles over his eyes and peered at the mall parking lot across the street for a full minute. Then he continued. "Thank you for taking the trouble to speak with me. My name is Gerald Kurt Paine. Please call me Gary. And yours?"

I told him my name and we shook hands. It appeared

that the nails had been torn from his fingers a long time ago, allowing other things to grow, but his hands were clean.

Gary asked me if I wanted to buy a pencil. I told him sure and gave him my only money, a five-dollar bill, my lunch money. He handed me a well-sharpened yellow HB pencil, just like the kind we gave the children at school.

Gary removed his goggles and stared at the sky for a long minute. He watched a tiny Cessna make a lazy turn towards the airport, scratched under his helmet, and then asked a different question. "Do you want to know the reason why I wear this helmet, young man — besides protection from falling pumpkins and wanted posters, I mean?"

"You like Nazi stuff," I said, and shrugged. It was a stupid and possibly hurtful answer, and I knew it.

Gary smiled and said, "I'm going to tell you." He looked for the airplane, but it was gone. "Wearing this helmet keeps other people safe from me. Whenever I take it off, people around me have nervous breakdowns and their negative thoughts and feelings get into my brain." He took off the helmet and searched my face, looking for signs of a nervous breakdown or negative thought waves, and then spoke again. "I think we can be friends. My last friend died in 1941. No, that is not quite correct. My *best* friend died in 1941, and the love of my life died not long after that, in 1944."

With that Gary strode away, not having told me the answer to his initial question. For some strange reason I felt honoured that my brainwaves had not affected him and that I had not suffered a breakdown.

The next day, a Wednesday, Gary Paine waved to me from his corner where the highway off-ramp met Fairway Road and gestured for me to park and come over. We met like old friends and shook hands.

He said, "That date I threw at you yesterday, Mr. History Teacher. Did you rush to your school library and grab an extra-thick, leather-bound, almost-never-used encyclopedia?"

I chuckled and said to the man wearing the heavy steel helmet, "I did. And I couldn't find a thing about that date, so I asked the school librarian. She had no idea either, so I found the head of our history department. She got upset, stared at me, and suggested that I return my history degree to the University of Toronto marked 'unused and unwarranted.'"

Gary Paine became very serious. He tightened the strap on the old helmet and tapped the steel with his knuckles a few times, a nervous gesture I was soon to know very well. Never again did I see the man without that steel wave-buster covering his belfry. "And?" he asked.

I was anxious not to disappoint my new friend. "The head of history told me that it was the beginning of one of the greatest periods in British history. And that Winston Churchill, the prime minister of Great Britain at the time, said that a lot was owed to those involved. I can't remember the exact quote, sorry. That was what she told me, so the next thing I did was go after school to the university, where I found books about the Battle of Britain. I wept when I read about what you and those others did."

Gary squinted into the sky and then turned his arms into airplane wings. With the flying goggles firmly in place, he flew around the parking lot making machine-gun noises. He landed near me and said proudly, "'Never was so much owed by so many to so few,' Churchill said that on August 20, 1940, after the most gruesome air battle in the history of the world. I was there. I know."

Clearly nervous, he tapped his helmet a few times,

probably remembering those months of do-or-die aerial warfare — or perhaps he had seen a few soul-suckers on his flight around the Walmart parking lot. "Yes, that was quite a day and quite a time. Maybe one day I'll tell you all about it, my new friend, teacher in a school with an orange-peel history curriculum."

I gave him a five-dollar bill for coffee and lunch and returned to my car.

Five days a week for the next forty years, I spent fifteen minutes every morning, Monday to Friday, talking with my friend. What did we talk about? Most days, nothing of real consequence, but on other days I was spellbound by the cryptograms of his life that he offered up. I learned quickly that Gary's brain no longer viewed his life as an orderly sequence of events, but rather as juxtapositions of emotions and colours and memories unhindered by time and space. Every day I listened, gave him a fiver, and then went on with my life.

Witness

On Friday, November 10, 2017, Gary Paine asked me if I would like to visit him the following day, because he had something to tell me and something to ask of me. I agreed and arrived with coffee, doughnuts, and muffins.

Gary lived under a bridge in a large cardboard box covered with thick, dark-coloured plastic. I handed him his double-double and he took two chocolate-glazed doughnuts while I had my bran muffin with raisins. He said nothing as he sat down carefully on the ground, tightening the straps of his steel helmet. I took a seat opposite on a large concrete block. On that beautiful, warm November day I waited for my friend, whom I had grown to love and respect, to begin.

Gary was ninety-eight years old, but he looked much younger that day. The puckered scar around his neck, however, seemed to glow as he finished the last crumbs of doughnut and drained his coffee. He sighed, added the empty cup to a long sleeve of other empty cups, and wiped his hands on his pants. Then he grasped my hand in a death grip and pulled me towards him in a desperate gesture that I had never seen before. I remember the smell of the double-double on his breath.

After a minute or so he said, "I am tired of it all and I want to die. But I would like to tell my story before I die. Will you be my witness? Will you bear witness and affirm the truths and lies of my life?"

I did not respond to his comment about impending death, because that was not my business. Instead I replied, "Gary, I would be honoured to be your witness, to listen and learn. Sir, you honour me with this request." I am generally not an emotional man, but I began to cry for my friend of forty years. He touched my shoulder and we cried together.

Gary tightened his grip on my hand so I could not let go. He pulled me closer and whispered, "I have a further thing to ask of you. Will you please write it all down so others will know? I want others to understand. Please?"

"Of course," I whispered back to the man sitting by his home next to old beer bottles and other crap.

Gary nodded, tapped the German helmet seven times, and said, "Thank you. It is a lot to ask." He sat for a long time after that, staring sadly towards the east.

I gently disengaged my hand from his, stood up, wiped the muffin crumbs from my pants, and went home to prepare for hockey practice with my grandson.

x x x

We met from nine o'clock in the morning until noon for the next fifty-two Saturdays. He talked and I wrote. When he had finished his story, I was a changed man.

"I am a self-proclaimed mumble-crust." That was the first thing Gary said to me on the first Saturday as we settled into our morning coffee on a bench intended for bus travellers, he as raconteur and I as witness. "Do you know what a mumble-crust person does, teacher?" he asked.

I had learned to give the man a five-count after a question, because generally his probes were aimed at himself. He said, "A crust that mumbles? Well, it is a dry food, of course, like these doughnut bits finding a place around my mouth and all over my shirt — yours too." He chuckled. "The homeless, the crazy, and the old all have this in common. So, as I talk and eat doughnuts for the next year, please excuse some of the crumbs that I will spill." He winked. "After all, my friend, I am all three of those things."

Gary scrutinized my eyes and then said, "Or I'm just crusty and mumble a lot." The laugh this time, however, held none of his previous humour.

"Well, where do I begin my tale of woe? I suppose the best place is an account of my very first memories as a child — wait, hold it a minute! First, I want to say something about truth, and it is this: I am a disturbed, destroyed man who lives in a world that is insane and inhabited by ghouls. I cannot exist within the confines of a world that is nuts, wacko, insane, and screwy, so I live on its fringes looking inwards, like so many others." He pointed down the street. People were emerging from the shadows of an overpass, pushing or pulling or simply carrying their belongings.

Gary continued. "And I am dangerous. Remember that as I tell my story — that I said I am dangerous. You will see why."

I waited more than five seconds, then replied, "Ah, but Gary, surely the truth of one's life is clouded and opaque, because of time and other things, is it not?" I was trying my best to sound intelligent, but I immediately wished I had remained mute. I still cannot believe that I used the phrase *one's life*.

Gary became agitated. He said, "Next time when you want to say something, don't — think before you say something stupid like that. You're not at university any more. This is the real world, where truth matters very much, not mumbo-jumbo theoretical bullshit. It's always best to listen." My friend stopped and shook his head for a moment, then continued. "Yup, for sure. Listening takes courage for sure, for a certainty. Listening is learning, and learning is a brave adventure that can be the shuck-and-jive that will keep the evil, the darkness, and the monsters at bay. So, listen and learn, okay? That, younger man than me, is another truth." Gary shook his head again, perhaps sorting the truth from the lies.

I mumbled, "Sorry, Gary."

I thought I would hear no more that day, but Gary Paine startled me by saying, "The truth ... What a concept! I believe that the first thing out of a person's mouth must be truth, or all else spewed out that day will be based on that initial lie. What I will tell you now is not bullshit. We have a few minutes and a bit of coffee to drink, so let us begin."

Gary's Story

I am. I saw. I suffered. I am damned. They are real. Aren't they?

Sometimes I believe that God is an asshole, but that isn't fair, because she is merely our absent landlord. My story is really a tale about an unrepentant Nazi, and he was a true asshole. You will find nothing about me, my exploits, and my tough times in any of the history books, the official records, or that YouTuber stuff, because anything and everything about me has been erased. I have been a ghost — and worse — since September 1945. You will soon learn why.

We will begin this story in the now when. The first thing you must do is get that Youtubey device thing on your hand-phoney computer and look for this: "The Russian Sleep Experiment." The writing will state that in the late 1940s, using a special gas and so on, the Soviets kept five prison inmates awake for fifteen straight days. Those men were given food and all the modern conveniences, except beds. The pictures show what happened to the prisoners. It's all nonsense, of course. But have a look at those people — a good long, hard look. They are pictures of very evil-looking hunched, fang-toothed, foul creatures dressed in the clothes of long-dead Egyptian mummies. And the eyes — look at the eyes.

You cannot picture it but trust me when I tell you that I was and continue to be a very good-looking man, despite the scars. In my youth, before I went to war, I was very popular with the ladies. However, inside my brain, underneath this heavy steel German World War II helmet that I wear, I am the creature that disgusted you when you opened that website and stared at the sleep-deprived monsters.

I am like a coin that I will describe for you later in

my diatribe: one side looks good, while the flipside is not so pretty. On the surface I am a handsome homeless man sitting on a bench watching people as they fret their way through life, while inside, deep within what is left of my soul, I am a *Nachzehrer*, an eater of souls, and as ugly and disfigured as the sleepless. The Nazi steel over my head is the barrier that keeps the monster within inside. There is enough irony there that even the stupid cannot miss.

I told my teacher friend that I give people nervous breakdowns. Bah! I used that term to hide what really happens when the hat comes off, because I didn't want to scare my new friend right off. (Once upon a time I had a good friend named MacDonald, and he would have said that pun was lame.) True enough. Anyway, about the steel barrier that I wear most days. When I remove my hat, the monster within feeds on the people around me, on the incipient terror and depression that lurk in the hearts of most people, just as that bastard in that prison long ago fed from me. He was my father, my teacher, and my executioner, and he ate my soul. Now whenever I remove this metal chapeau, I devour the hopelessness of others. It is very important that you understand this about me.

The day I met my new friend, back in 1978, I removed my helmet for a moment because I was hungry, and people in their early twenties are always insecure and pathetic, easy to destroy — I should know. But we talked and I liked him very much, and he gave me a reason to be a little more human. His heart was pure and he was a kind and generous man, so I did not feel the urge to feed from him. I replaced my helmet and have loved this man, my only friend, for the past forty years.

However, my friend and his kind heart did not cure me, because the need to devour was permanently annealed in my essence when I was the forgotten prisoner, executed, revived, and then reconstructed. Now I live in a cardboard cage under a bridge, and it is the perfect environment for a soul-sucker with a Nazi war-helmet insulator.

Ah, enough of that. Let us go back to happier times, to when I was a very young man and knew everything and had the confidence and the ability to take on any project. I was so stupid, but so brave and enterprising. Most people blame their childhood for any success or failure in life, or the things that did or did not happen to them as kids. But me, I loved my childhood, especially when I was eighteen, so let's start there. We can blame it all on Jenny, or perhaps because I lived in an area settled by German immigrants, or maybe we can blame my excellent German.

Jenny, My Love

Falling from an airplane at a thousand feet without a parachute will kill you every time. Our town, originally named after a city in Germany, boasted a large fairground on the south side of the city, near the Grand River. Barns and stalls and a wide half-mile horse track were the pride and joy of the community. The fall fair was the time when the grounds came alive, when the farming community came to show and sell and the city slickers came to see and buy. Every year we counted on something different and exciting to happen at our fair, and 1936 was no exception.

It was September and I was eighteen years old, with a few dollars in my pocket from selling a calf I had raised from birth. Colourful posters around town were advertising a barnstorming exhibition and airplane rides in a JN-4 Curtiss Jenny, built in 1917 and perhaps used in the Great War, so the writing stated. The fine print proclaimed that it had been built in Canada and so was called a JN-4

Jenny Canuck. I didn't believe that, of course, but I wanted a ride!

When I arrived at the grounds, the Jenny had been flying in circles around the town, drumming up business. When the beautiful creature landed and stopped next to the horse track, a line quickly formed of people looking for a ride, with me at the front. The pilot unfastened a complex jumble of belts and harness, lowered his flying goggles, and jumped, somewhat awkwardly, to the ground. His face was covered in dirt and oil, and when he spoke to the crowd, his voice had the slur of a drunk.

The pilot raised his arms and addressed me, the first person in line. He said, "Young man, I am Arthur, King of the Barnstormers and the last member of the Flying Circus. I bid you hello." Arthur pointed to the airplane, which was ticking loudly as it cooled. "This pretty machine is Jennifer, my trusty steed. We offer a circuit of the town for a dollar or, for five dollars, a circuit of the town upside down — as we say in the flying business, inverted." He turned the palm of his hand to the sky and burped.

In those days everybody drove a car with a pint of whisky between their knees. I thought that flying couldn't be more difficult than driving, so I handed the knight my five dollars. Surely there were no rules about drinking and flying. The pilot stuffed the fiver under a three-quarters-empty pint of rye whisky jammed into the front pocket of his aviation coveralls. Then King Arthur belted and harnessed me into the front seat of Jennifer and explained what the various controls did and did not do. I was very confused. Then he jumped into the back seat and fastened his own set of restraints.

"Oh, shit," he shouted from the back, and went through the ritual of undoing the various clasps and fastenings again. "Sorry, I need to take a piss," he yelled over his shoulder as he ran for a washroom.

Back again, he jumped into the rear and signalled a volunteer to spin the propeller and then step aside. We taxied to the far end of the open field, where Arthur gunned the throttle. The ninety-horsepower engine took us faster and faster down that makeshift runway. I was watching the wings when they suddenly flexed upwards and took the full weight of the aircraft. We climbed steadily into the air — it was the second greatest thrill I would have that day. We flew right side up for a complete circle of the town. Then, approaching the fairgrounds, Arthur yelled something and inverted the Jenny.

It was fun. We flew upside down for a few seconds in perfect harmony, me laughing and shouting from the sheer thrill of the experience. I stopped laughing when the Jenny began to bob and weave as if out of control. I looked back to see what the Flying Circus guy was doing, because I was scared — but he was gone. He had forgotten to buckle himself into his seat when he returned from the washroom and was now on his way to the ground.

Part of my mind went into silly mode. I was upside down in an airplane and was about to die but laughed because things falling down looked to me like they were going up. The drunk who had put me into that situation seemed to be taking a fast track to the moon, twisting and flailing his arms and legs. It was very funny — for a few seconds.

I did nothing at first as the upside-down Jenny began to nose towards the ground, all the while inverted. I had a hard case of the woulda-shouldas and wanted to be home having a beer on the front porch. That was not to be, so I decided to live.

Gently I pushed the stick to the right. The beautiful creature, holding me close to her bosom, responded; we rotated to right side up and then around to upside down again. I let her continue the rotation until we were right side up again and then moved the stick to the neutral position. The wings were lined up with the horizon, but the nose dipped towards the ground again. That was bad, so I pulled the stick into my stomach. The nose rose, that's for sure, but the airplane climbed for a bit and then slowed down. When the wings started to shake, I knew I was in trouble again, so I pushed the stick forward. The plane picked up speed and dove for the ground, so I pulled the stick again, but gently this time, and the Curtiss Jenny began to fly nicely.

I was sweating and scared and wondering what to do next when I heard a young woman's voice saying, *Land anywhere, now.*

It made sense to reduce the power, so I pulled the throttle back quite a bit but not all the way. The propeller slowed and again the nose dropped, somewhat less dramatically than before. I fiddled with the stick until the Jenny was descending less acutely. I was relieved, so I decided to let the aircraft descend on her own and see what happened. It was then that I realized that the bar on the floor turned the nose left or right, so, using the rudder bar, I edged Jennifer towards an open field about a mile from our farm.

I was afraid to touch the throttle again and was relieved when we cleared a large elm tree at the end of that field. Once past the tree, I figured it was time to pull the throttle all the way back, and of course the nose dropped. The Jenny was about to smack into the field and kill me. I did not know what to do, but the stick inched towards me a bit, the nose lifted and the wheels contacted the ground first. The stupid thing had no brakes, but it stopped just before hitting the trees at the other end of the field.

I laughed and screamed with joy because I was alive.

As I watched the propeller spin slowly in front of me, I came up with a plan. I quickly understood that I could steer the beautiful creature on the ground with the rudder bar, so I pushed the throttle gently forward and drove her along the edge of that field of newly cut hay, towards the gate. Once at the gate, I throttled all the way back. The little aircraft sat staring at the road, as docile as a puppy. Once the gate was open, with the throttle slightly forward we edged our way onto the road and headed towards our farm, all the while steering with my feet.

At the first stop sign I checked for traffic and noticed a tractor and hay wagon lumbering along the road in our direction. The kids in the wagon hooted and hollered as they passed in front of me, but the man driving the tractor, the city's mayor, did not turn his head. He was intent on keeping his crop safe and sound.

At our farm at last, I reined in my steed in front of an unused barn. I stopped the engine, pushed her into the barn, shut the door, and laughed in the pure wonder of it — and because I had just committed larceny. They found the broken body of the pilot near the fairground, but not his airplane.

Flying Is Easy

Well, I learned to dismantle that plane and then reassemble it and dismantle it and reassemble it again. It wasn't that much different from a tractor or the old car we owned. Where I found an obvious flaw or damage, I simply made a new part out of whatever I could find around the farm. In no time the walls of the barn were cluttered with diagrams and drawings.

My one and only landing had been mostly luck, so I

had to learn to fly the Jenny properly. Just before Christmas that year, I convinced Mom and Pop not to plant corn down the middle of one of our fields in the spring. It was an interesting conversation.

I got my dad his third beer and said, "Pop, I found something interesting a few weeks back."

Dad sipped his beer and looked over his seed catalogue at me. All children know that look. All he said was "And?"

"Well, Pop, it's real big and I stored it in that barn we don't use much except to store junk and stuff. The one in the back, near that copse of maple trees."

His catalogue was on the table by then, because he knew me well. I was one of those precocious children who, even at eighteen, are both loved and feared by their parents. "Where did you find this thing that is stored in our unused barn near that stand of sugar maples?" I could not help but notice that he asked *where* before he asked *what*.

I sipped my fourth beer and said, "Well, Dad, that's the funny thing. I found it in the sky near the fairgrounds."

My mother piped up then. "In the sky, you say?" She dried her hands on her red apron and sat beside her husband, my father. I had her full attention.

"Um, I took an airplane ride at the fair back in the fall."

"And the nice pilot gave you his airplane because you were such a good passenger?" my mom asked sarcastically.

I looked at both parents and asked, "Don't you remember hearing about the pilot who fell from his plane that day?"

Mom and Dad didn't get out much. They answered in unison, "No."

I decided it was time to tell them how I had ended up in the front seat of the Jenny that day. I omitted the bit about just missing the elm tree.

My mom asked, "So the idiot named his airplane Jenny. Why would he do that?"

"I don't know, Mom, but it's a Curtiss Jenny."

My mom was shocked that an airplane would have a name. She asked, "The pilot who fell from the sky — leaving you, a mere boy, alone in the plane — gave it a man's name too?"

"No, Mom. The factory people or the inventor named it the Curtiss Jenny Canuck."

"That's just outlandish. A girl-boy airplane?" my mom said. Then she asked, "So you stole the thing and hid it in our barn?'

"Yes, Mom, I did, because I figured the pilot wouldn't need it anymore," I said, hoping my little joke would help with the next topic.

"There is one more thing," I said, looking at my father, who did not seem at all upset that we now owned a 1917 Curtiss biplane with a funny name, albeit stolen from a dead man.

"I knew there would be. I've just been waiting to hear what it is."

"Um, I'm going to learn to fly it. Can you please not plant corn down the middle of the field behind the trees, so I can build a landing strip? I only need a bit of land, about three hundred feet long and twenty-five feet wide. Please, Dad?"

The late 1930s were still reeling from the effects of the Great Depression, and every acre counted if we were to survive as farmers. I knew that and my parents knew that.

My dad laughed and said, "Son, of course. But do not tell anyone about the plane, not ever. If for some reason you leave this farm and do not take your Jenny, make it disappear. That is my one condition." With that my parents went to bed. I could hear them laughing about their eccentric child, but later that night I heard my father having one of his nightmares.

The corn grew to the edge of and around the strip of land designated as my landing area. I spent hours driving my Jenny up and down that strip, steering with my feet on the rudder bar.

The next thing I did was get a copy of the Curtiss JN-4 Jenny Canuck manual, but it was almost useless. It talked about weight and horsepower and wisely advised making sure it had gas and oil. The best advice, written at the top of the document, was to examine it all over to see if things looked okay.

Taking off into the wind I already knew about, but eventually I found something useful. I remember exactly what it said: "After attaining a few feet of headway, raise the tail with the controls and keep it in this position to prevent the machine from leaving the ground until it is well past its minimum flying speed." I did not know that lifting the tail was important and worried about the minimum flying speed, because the booklet did not give a specific number. I decided to play that part by feel when the time came to launch into the blue — or perhaps, if things went badly, into the black. Another interesting thing was written under a section titled "Steering." It stated that once in the air the best way to turn the aircraft was by using the ailerons with help from the rudder bar. I remember going "Aha!"

One morning, after eating a large plate of German sausage and scrambled eggs topped off with a cup of very strong coffee, I decided to give it a try. The plan was to go with full power for a few seconds, jump briefly into the air, and then reduce the power and gently settle back down onto the earth. With a brisk wind coming straight at me, it was full power and off we went.

Are you at all familiar with Burns — Robert, from Scotland? That bastard had the truth of it when he wrote:

But, Mousie, thou art no thy-lane,
In proving *foresight* may be vain:
The best laid schemes o' *Mice* an' *Men*
    Gang aft agley,
An' lea'e us nought but grief an' pain,
    For promis'd joy!

Of course, my scheme went to shit that fine morning. I roared down the runway — no doubt scaring those mice with their morning plans — at full power and tail up and fifty miles per hour. Rather than fly a bit and then down again, I became so excited that I forgot to take the power back to idle. Jenny climbed steadily higher and higher; I kept it between fifty and sixty and that was okay. I levelled off at what seemed a million feet and realized that full power was not necessary when flying level. I took my Jenny in a big, very gentle circle to the left, using the ailerons, and headed for my runway. I then reduced power, kept the wings level and the front lined up with the runway (using the rudder bar), and landed, having remembered to bring the nose up a bit before touchdown. It was the highlight of my life. I was into the blue!

The next day I removed the old paint with sandpaper and painted my Jenny bright orange, with a white skull over crossbones on the underside of the lower wings. When the paint had dried, Jenny and I began our grand adventures together, over the town and into the country-side. We buzzed barns and homes, landed in newly cut hay fields (to the dismay of farmers), and flew beside cars and trucks travelling along the country roads and lanes. People usually pointed and waved, but sometimes we would earn shouts and a shaken fist directed at the man in the orange airplane who was flying so recklessly.

My beautiful Jenny and I became a hot topic at the

local hardware store and the barber shop. I wondered aloud while getting my hair cut if it was the ghost of the drunken pilot looking for the bottle of rye whisky he had lost. After a while, as the story became more embellished, many people swore that bullshit was true, and other stories emerged. The headless pilot who had forgotten to dodge the propeller blade but was still able to take off was my favourite version. On October 31, just before dark, I flew around and around the town trying to drop rotten pumpkins onto the city streets. Unfortunately, I hit a couple of houses and cars and scared some witches shuffling along the sidewalk.

The pumpkin bombing and smashing created quite a furore with the city fathers. A town meeting was called and a reward was offered for the identification, capture, and punishment of the person or persons responsible for scaring children and causing property damage on Halloween night. Posters were nailed to trees and posts and people were asked to note where the ghost plane landed and to report sightings and/or information to the local police or members of the town council.

The poster was excellent. My airplane was drawn from below, with the bones stark against the orange paint; a perfect pumpkin was drawn on one side of Jenny and a headless man on the other. I collected as many of those wanted posters as possible and stuck up a signed copy in the shed where I kept Jenny. The following Saturday afternoon the stolen posters were loaded into the front seat of the airplane and I headed downtown at a hundred feet above the ground. When everyone's attention had turned skyward, I inverted the Jenny and the posters fluttered down.

Perhaps that was taking things too far again, but I was young and carefree, untroubled by life and full of vitality and positivity. However, to be safe, I kept Jenny in the barn until spring. During the winter I removed the orange paint and outfitted her in a beautiful sky blue with yellow flowers.

A Tomb for Jenny

It was early May 1939. War was coming and I wanted to help, but I wanted to help by being a Spitfire pilot. Or if I couldn't pilot a Spitfire, I decided a Hawker Hurricane would be fine. That meant getting to England and then somehow convincing somebody to trust me with their large, dangerous machines. And so I started on my great adventure in the spring of 1939.

The first problem was my Jenny — I remembered what my father had said. I loved that machine and what it had taught me about life and about myself. I decided to become an aircraft vivisectionist. I fired up the woodstove in my shop where I kept Jenny safe from the weather and ghost hunters. Then I dismantled and labelled each part of that beautiful machine, down to the smallest piece. I wanted the entire thing to fit into a few large containers, even the wings. Each piece was greased and carefully wrapped in oilcloth.

Finally, I used the tractor to dig a large hole in the middle of that field where my parents had allowed me to build a landing strip. In she went, and I buried her with fine Ontario topsoil. I placed a few large granite boulders on top so I could locate her again and planted four small oak trees next to the rocks: north, east, south, and west. The job was done and the Jenny had been put to rest.

After the war I was going to resurrect my ghost, fly around town, and scare all the kids. After that I would fly across North America, giving rides, drinking coffee, and talking about the war. It was a wonderful fantasy.

Car Payments

Hello. Owner of the red Mustang here. I am interrupting Gary's story at the beginning of his narrative to tell you about a conversation I had this week with my wife.

She had no idea that I had been making "car payments" for forty years to a man with a very heavy steel World War II military helmet, old flying goggles, and a faded, once blue Royal Air Force uniform. It had been my secret, a thing I had begun before I met her at school. I was the history teacher and she taught geography, so it was a perfect match — a friendly game of Trivial Pursuit was always fun.

Gary was my secret, but since I had agreed to be his witness every Saturday morning for fifty-two weeks, I decided Mary should know. I picked up a very nice bottle of red wine on the way home from work on Friday, made supper, and remembered not to chill the wine.

My wife arrived home and her first words were, "All right, what have you done? Speeding ticket? New golf clubs? An affair? What? You never make supper, and this wine is expensive. Besides, you don't like red wine."

I sighed and said, "No to all of the above, but I need to tell you something that I have kept to myself for a while. It's something I started before I met you and it just kept going."

"You stole money?"

"In a way, yes."

I poured the wine, but we never ate supper that day. I told her about my forty years of meetings with a homeless man named Gary Paine and how I had spent quite a bit of our money on him. I told Mary about the man's request and how I had agreed to write his story.

Mary cried on my shoulder, told me I was the best human ever born, and kissed me. Then we went upstairs. Ever practical, she first turned off the stove and grabbed the half-finished bottle.

On the Rails

After putting Jenny into the ground, I realized I hadn't a clue about how to get to England. I was young — which really meant naive and impulsive — so I decided to wing it. It was the latter part of the Dirty Thirties, and the Great Depression had its icy fingers up everybody's ass. Lots of folks were still riding the rails back then, looking for work, and my first idea was to jump onto a boxcar on its way to Toronto. My second idea was better.

The train station on the corner of Weber and King Streets, near downtown, was old even then, having been constructed in 1897. That majestic building, which is used a lot less today, was the hub that connected our town to the rest of the world via the Grand Trunk Railway, as we continued to call the Canadian Pacific and Canadian National rail companies. Duffel bag over my shoulder, I stood looking at the schedule for trains to Toronto and prepared to execute my plan.

In those days train conductors were on the lookout for freeloaders, so the main thing was to get onto the train and have the ticket master think you belonged there. I combed my hair and straightened my tie and then picked up a discarded used ticket and folded it just so. I waited for a large group to board the train, flashed my ticket, and pretended to be with a mother and three daughters who were going to Toronto, animated about their shopping trip. The conductor gave my ticket a quick glance as I boarded with the unsuspecting family. I was now on the train bound for Toronto, but the difficult part would be to stay on the train. Train conductors back then had a bad habit of getting passengers to prove their worth.

I took a seat in the front of the car, facing the rear door, and watched. When the sullen man in the company suit and hat began to stroll down the aisle towards me, asking to see tickets, I pretended to be ill and made a beeline to the tiny washroom between the cars. I made vomiting noises until I heard the man pass from our car to the next, and then I went back to my seat and fell asleep. I awoke as the locomotive pulled into Union Station in Toronto. As I stepped onto the platform, the conductor asked if I was feeling better. I felt like a jerk as I made my way to Front Street.

I wandered up and down Front Street and Lakeshore Boulevard, bought and ate a poke of hot chestnuts, and finally found my way back to Union Station, wondering what to do next. Enquiring about trains heading east, I was told that none were going that way for at least a day, for security reasons. Then the official chuckled and pointed to a huge blue locomotive with six cars behind it. He said, "Now, boy, the beauty over there is headed that way soon, nonstop to Montreal. But you can't get a ticket for that one."

The train the man had referred to was being loosely guarded by two Royal Canadian Mounted Policemen, who were chatting and smoking. I watched for an hour until I figured out their routine. It was to walk around the train in opposite directions every twenty minutes or so, meet in front of the engine and have a smoke, chat some more, and repeat. I watched them make another circuit just to be sure. As soon as they lit up the next time, I dashed between the end two cars and entered the last car through a side door, which I was very pleased to find unlocked. Inside, the car was empty except for two large, ornate tables and half a dozen uncomfortable-looking chairs. It was late, so I crawled under the largest table and fell asleep, using my duffel bag as a pillow.

At six in the morning the train jerked into action as it began its journey to Montreal. My head fell off the duffel bag and smacked onto the floor. At the same time I felt the toe of a pointed shoe kick me gently in the ribs. A voice followed on the heels of the toe jab.

"Well, well, what have we here? A young stowaway, I am thinking."

I scrambled out from under the table as fast as I could, more embarrassed than scared. I had intended to wake up in the night and find a better place to hide. "A stowaway?" I asked. "Yes, sir. I'm trying to get to Montreal so I can get on a ship to England and then join the Royal Air Force to fly Spitfires. I'm twenty."

The man laughed and said, "Well then, you are on the correct train, young man, because this exact train is now on its way, without stopping, to Montreal, Quebec. You, sir, have chosen the correct conveyance to precipitate your grand adventure. Please have a seat. Would you care for some hot oatmeal, or buttered toast, perhaps? Coffee? I will ring my butler forthwith."

Munching on hot buttered toast and enjoying the best coffee I had ever tasted, I asked, "Are you English, from England?"

My host chuckled and then laughed aloud. "Why, I suppose I am both. I was born in a cottage in England and my accent is that of one of its regions."

I glanced about the car and saw wealth and privilege in the fine carpet, the oil paintings, the luxurious furniture. To me they were well suited for a fancy parlour, like that special room in every house back home that would be used only if the King or someone important visited. "Is this your train?" I asked.

"This magnificent train does not belong to me, but it is mine to use until I leave for home," he replied. He reached into the top drawer of a small desk I had not noticed earlier and removed a pack of Chesterfield cigarettes and some long wooden matches. Except when he fell asleep later that day, from then on he was not without a cigarette in his hand — plus one or two nesting contentedly in one of many ornate ashtrays scattered about the room. I refused an offered smoke. I had heard they were good for clearing the lungs, but my lungs were fine and didn't need a boost.

My host stubbed a half-smoked cigarette into an ashtray and offered his hand, saying, "How rude of me, my young stowaway and travelling companion. Introductions are in order. My friends call me Bertie, and since we are already friends, please feel free to use that name. I have other names, but they are mere *noms de plume*, so to speak."

We shook as new friends and fellow travellers. I gave him my name in full and he repeated it. Then he looked at his watch and surprised me by saying, "By Jove, do you know what time it is in London, in England?"

The math was easy and I had a watch. I replied, "Eleven-thirty in the morning, I believe."

"You are correct, Gary. It is after eleven, and that is just the right time for our first gin and tonic." He called for his butler and ordered a bottle. Within minutes, two crystal glasses, a very large bottle of gin, and a decanter of tonic were placed quietly on the table. The man wore a complete butler's outfit, with a dark suit and white gloves.

"To your health and success in the Royal Air Force," Bertie said in his upper-class drawl. Then he coughed violently and spat into a white handkerchief. He had the good manners not to look at its contents.

As that wonderful train made headway to Montreal, I learned to appreciate the wonders of Mother Gin. Years later, when I became a drunk living in a crystal cave, it was gin I drank or nothing at all, and my first drink each day was a toast to that kind and generous man.

By noon Toronto time (five o'clock England time), we were drunk, and talkative as only intoxicated people can be. I asked Bertie what he did for a living and how he had become so rich. He smiled a very sad smile and told me this: "Gary, my brother David should be sitting here in this luxurious train, not me, but the bugger quit the family business and ran away to America. When my mother told me that his job, with all its responsibilities and pressures, had become mine, I ran from the room. My wife was waiting for me in the hallway. Elizabeth, calm as always, swept me into her arms. I wept as I held her and told her that I was sorry, that it would not be the life together we had planned. She lifted my head from her bosom and told me that she would help me become the leader I needed to be. And, my friend, she has done just that. Elizabeth is everything to me. It was she who convinced me of the necessity of this long, boring trip. Perhaps you can meet her later; she is in the next car playing poker with some of our friends."

"I'm sorry," I whispered and reached over to the gold tray to pour us both another gin and tonic. "And I would be honoured to meet such a wonderful lady."

Bertie continued. "I am going to stay in London when the war comes and not run away and hide. That is why I'm going home now. Elizabeth will stay there with me, and our daughters as well. Gary, I am very worried about this war that is coming from the east." He had a habit of changing subjects mid-conversation. "Chamberlain is not the man to lead when the enemy is at our door. He lacks the cunning and the ruthlessness we will need when that madman threatens. I can think of only one man who can do that for us and I can't bear his self-righteous ways. You can never predict what he will say or what he will do."

With that he stretched out on the couch and fell asleep for a few minutes. Then he suddenly sat up and dashed off to the next car. He returned in about five minutes and handed me a note with instructions. With that he fell asleep again until the train slowed for its final approach to Montreal.

I stepped out of that beautiful train before it stopped, to avoid the very large crowd that seemed to be waiting for my friend. Before I did, Bertie stopped me for a brief second and handed me a second envelope. In it were one hundred Canadian dollars and one hundred English pounds. He said, "My friend, I wish you well in your aspirations, but I fear for you, because you carry a certain melancholy about you — a dark foreshadowing, if you will."

I nodded my thanks, thinking the same about my friend, and hoping that he would find the right man to run his business.

Soul-Sucking

Yesterday I approached a very young man sitting in one of those coffee shops with striped awnings that seem to inhabit every street corner. I had left the steel helmet and goggles tucked into my grocery cart in the parking lot, where it was easy for me to see. I could see that the man had been sitting at his place for some time; his coffee had that cold, neglected look and the butter on his raisin muffin had begun to congeal.

"Mind if I sit here?" I asked, coffee and chocolate doughnut in hand, and sat down at his table.

The man nodded his acceptance of my intrusion and moved his plate closer to his coffee cup. He took a sip of his drink and grimaced.

"Sometimes cold coffee is as bad as a cold heart," I murmured, just loudly enough for the man to hear. I thought he agreed, judging by his quick laugh. "You agree?" I asked.

His answer was not as expected. "It depends, doesn't it. Some people like things in life to be cold and others hot. But I know this: Cold always draws its energy from hot. It is the way of the universe. Hot cannot draw energy from cold. Is that not so? Aren't you a homeless man trying to draw energy from me?"

I was terrified because I had forgotten to wear my goggles and an eidolon had found me, and I had found him. He was still talking. "But can colder draw energy from less cold? The question here is, who is which? Einstein would have called it relative. Am I right, brother?"

I got up to leave because I knew the answer to that question. The young man with the cold coffee grasped my arm and pulled me back into my seat. It was then that I realized he was wearing a badly torn uniform with a tiny Niagara Falls pin attached to the lapel of his shirt. He pushed his cup in front of me and I lifted it off the table and sipped the contents. It was not coffee, nor was it cold. The man pointed to his many injuries — the source of the hot liquid. I said nothing and drank the remainder of the sanguine fluid. I smiled because I knew the identity of the man sitting with the congealed butter, although we had never been formally introduced.

The man then spoke in German. "You have been expecting me, Flying Officer Paine?" I nodded and shrugged. He also nodded, then continued. "Yes, our father was an unrepentant right-wing schizophrenic Nazi bastard, much like yourself, right?"

I replied, also in German, "He created monsters just like me, yes."

The man in the torn and burned uniform retrieved his mug and whispered, "You are a monster and Father was Doctor Frankenstein, and the world has chased you with firebrands and pitchforks. You lurch about and you feed, but *Vater* did not quite finish his creation, I think."

"I feel complete. I feed on the despair of others and now I wish to die. Ghoul, what do you want of me?" I whispered back.

"I have come to complete the job that *Vater* started. You have been expecting me, but hoping to avoid me with those silly spectacles."

"Yes, and yes." I stared longingly at my grocery cart, now being drenched with rain.

"Yes, and yes," the ghost repeated.

"Finish, so I can go," I said.

The man moved closer to me and looked at the muffin and the empty cup. Any humanity that I might have imagined he possessed disappeared from his face when he said, "Flying Officer Paine, our father wished me well when I left our home to travel to England that final morning. He had me play our song on my violin and he seemed almost content. Almost. His very final words to me were: 'Son, I love you, but do not come back to this place unless you stop your deviant ways. Perhaps battle with the English will make a man of you, will cure you.' Paine, you see, he really was a bastard. First he destroyed me, and then he destroyed you — us."

"I am sorry," I told the man's eidolon, and he nodded his thanks.

"But, Paine, I wanted to live. You destroyed my airplane, and that was war. When we were about to bail out, you killed us all with your machine gun, and that was murder. You kept shooting and shooting. The gunners were just boys, thrilled to be part of it all. My co-pilot was nineteen years old and had a wife and infant son in Munich, and the navigator had a loving mother waiting for her eighteen-year-old boy to return. That boy had a brilliant mind; his goal in life was not to kill the British but to become a physicist and discover the meaning of life. We were so young and wanted to live. We wanted life and happiness and fulfillment, like everybody else. Have you had a life of happiness, Paine, old chum? I think not. I think our *Vater* was right in what he did."

The coffee shop became very cold. Every patron in the room stood, turned towards me, and judged. Four young men had taken seats across from us and were staring through me, back to what could have been. I could not move, so I simply sat.

The dead German bomber pilot asked me a final question. "Why did you murder us, Paine?" I closed my eyes for a long moment, remembering that morning and how happy I had been with my kill that day. When I opened them again, the men were gone and the shop was again full of noise and warmth. My brother's empty cup and muffin had not moved, and the patrons were seated. But they continued to stare quietly in my direction, and some pointed.

Halifax Is a Long Way

The last time I was in Montreal was before the war and I had one hundred British pounds sterling and one hundred Canadian dollars. Let me think for a minute and do some very rough calculations. Today the hundred Canadian dollars would be worth somewhere between fifteen hundred and two thousand dollars, which is pretty good. The English money would be worth about six thousand dollars. The rich man on the fancy train had given a young man he'd just met around four hundred dollars — about eight thousand in today's money.

My memory of the prices of things in 1939 is a bit foggy, but I seem to remember that a fresh loaf of bread cost about five cents and a brand-new Ford automobile at the dealership went for about a thousand bucks, give or take. So that was a very generous gift from the gentleman who liked his travelling comforts, his cigarettes, and gin, and who loved his wife, Elizabeth, above all else.

Montreal became a terrifying place when I discovered that it was a French-speaking city. I wondered how this could be, since my Scottish high school teacher had explained, at some length, that this area of Canada had been conquered a while back by a Scottish army wearing kilts, at some fort on top of a hill. Surely, I reasoned, that would have given the conquered people enough time to pick up some English. The alternative was that my Scottish instructor was a madman and needed to cut down on the whisky before trying to influence bored young minds.

At lunch I asked a waiter who was willing to speak English if Quebec was a country separate from Canada. He said, "*Non, mon ami*, not yet, but in our hearts and souls *nous sommes nous*. We are Québécois." Ah, I reasoned, rebellion was stirring. I thought about guillotines, heads in baskets and knitting in the centre of town.

"Oh" was all I said. Then I asked if there was a passenger ship headed for England.

The Quebec separatist dissident laughed and said, "*Non, monsieur.* Likely none until the war that is coming ends." He thought for a moment and then told me that a large ocean liner was leaving from Halifax, Nova Scotia, sometime in the middle of June. I raced to a library and found a map of Canada, because I had no idea where Halifax, Nova Scotia, was and therefore no clue how far away it was and how I would get there.

I had ten days or so to make the journey. I read that they spoke mostly English in Halifax. With a piece of string I traced a route through Quebec and a place called New Brunswick, grasped the string at both ends and placed it along the distance calculator line at the bottom of the map. Then I said, "*Merde*" (just to fit in), when it became apparent that Halifax was seven hundred miles or more from Montreal. Magic trains were scarce, so I needed a plan. I thought about walking but realized it would take about a month if I was lucky.

I purchased a large *boussole* and located north and east. There was a big hill east of the city, and I decided to use that obvious landmark as the starting point for my journey to Halifax, Nova Scotia. That night I slept under an *arbre* at the base of the mountain, dreamed about my Jenny and hoped that one day I could resurrect that beautiful machine. I dreamt in German.

Next morning found me at the side of the road with a forlorn look and a sign that read *NEED RIDE TO HALIFAX*. Five o'clock found me at the same spot but looking far more forlorn, so I picked up my possessions and checked into a small motel. Lying on the bed, smelling stale urine and other things, I realized that I was a very stupid young man from rural Ontario.

Morning after that again found me standing by the road. My clothes and hair were clean and I was smiling. My sign this time read *NEED A RIDE TO ENGLAND TO JOIN THE ROYAL AIR FORCE. WILLING TO DIE FOR OUR FREEDOM.* Underneath the English was written *UN HOMME DE L'ONTARIO DOIT S'ÉVADER DE MONTRÉAL ET IL EST DÉSOLÉ QU'IL PARLE L'ANGLAIS. BONNE CHANCE AVEC LA RÉVOLU-TION.* The motel owner had been more than happy to help me with the French. I made it to Halifax in three days, well fed and all expenses paid.

There was indeed a passenger liner scheduled to leave Halifax harbour for Liverpool, England, on the evening of the fifteenth of June, but a very large sign, written in huge red letters, declared that tickets could no longer be purchased. Nevertheless, I was determined to gain passage on the *Empress of Britain* and I had a week to do it. I was twenty years old and knew that my first step was to find a hotel, book a room, go downstairs to the bar and drink beer until I was sick, then go back upstairs and sleep.

Downstairs there was a fistfight at the door to the bar between two drunk sailors and one sober civilian. The civilian was a talented fighter with some obvious training in martial combat, and in time he would have won the fight, but I was impatient to have a drink, so I joined the fray on the side of the civilian. With both arms windmilling about, I landed one punch and received two in the face and one in the stomach. We won the fight in no time and together headed for the bar, where my new friend ordered two beers each.

The hotel bar had an excellent view of the harbour and the beautiful cruise liner being loaded with cargo destined for England. My new friend and I drank our first beer quickly and introduced ourselves. His name was John MacDonald, from a town with a stupid name about thirty minutes east of my own. He instructed me to call him Mac, as John was his dad's name. Mac and I drank and drank. I told him about my Jenny and the great pumpkin smash of 1938, how I had made my way to Halifax harbour, and how I wanted to get to England so I could join the Royal Air Force and learn to fly Spits (or my second choice, Hurricanes) and be part of the impending war with Germany. I looked at the *Empress* as I talked, as if her lights in the darkness were daring me to try to board her.

Mac saw my look and laughed, then stated what was obvious. "So, you don't have a ticket then, I suppose."

I answered, "No. I never thought I wouldn't be able to buy a goddam ticket to a place about to enter a goddam war. I could understand that getting away from that place would be a problem, but getting to the place? It's silly."

MacDonald smiled and said, "The reason, old chum, that you can't get aboard is because the King of England and his wife will be sailing on her when it leaves in a few days. They and their friends, pages, butlers, cooks and such take up a lot of space."

"*Merde*," I said for the second time in my life, wondering if I could swim to the anchor chain and shinny up to the ship like a rat.

"I, on the other hand, own a third-class ticket on the *Empress of Britain*, headed for Liverpool, England, on June 15, 1939. See, it says so right here," MacDonald informed me, displaying his well-folded ticket on the beer-stained bar. "And all meals are included."

I got up to leave but Mac pulled me back down. "What?" I asked.

"Paine, my new friend who cannot ever expect to win

a fistfight on his own, I will tell you two and only two —
well, perhaps three — things about me. The first is that I
am twenty-eight years old and therefore smarter and more
experienced than you. The second is that I came first in
my class at law school at Osgoode Hall in Toronto." He
burped and shook his head and said, "Was that two or
three things I told you about me? Because I've been sworn
to secrecy about myself."

I held up two fingers and accidently answered in
German. "*Zwei*."

"You speak German?" he asked. I nodded.

MacDonald nodded back and said, "Well, I speak
France French. My wife lives in France, and that is where I
met her. I'll teach you a bit of *français* once we get aboard
— it might come in handy one day. Wait, that's five things
I've told you about me, plus the French thing. Time for
bed. I will see you here at noon tomorrow to hatch our
plan."

Not only did MacDonald have a great plan to get me
onto the *Empress of Britain*, we rehearsed with costumes
and props in the back room of the bar, well supplied with
beer and good Canadian whisky on ice. The man had a
talent for chicanery and the subterfuge that far outstripped
my own.

On June 15, 1939, at five o'clock in the afternoon, Mac
and I were positioned in the middle of a long line of very
nervous people about to board the ship. Mac wore a finely
tailored suit and carried his suitcase in his right hand,
where the ticket collector could see it; my canvas duffel
bag was tucked under his other arm. I was positioned
two people behind Mac, dressed as a merchant sailor and
carrying a small bucket and a rag, held low so the people
on board would not notice.

The ticket collector was stationed at the end of the

gangway on board the ship. He held out his hand, waiting for Mac's ticket. Mac sighed, placed his case and my bag on the deck near the ship's officer, and fumbled for his ticket. Finally locating it, he was about to place it into the outstretched hand when he pointed over the man's shoulder and yelled, "Look everybody, it's the King! Over there! There he goes. Is that the Queen with him? Oh my god, the King himself and Queen Elizabeth!"

Then he began to sing "God Save the King," and of course everybody joined him, twisting about to catch a glimpse of the monarch. Song and drama over, Mac handed the official his ticket, received his cabin key, and walked onto the deck, passing a tired sailor, bucket in hand, who was conscientiously cleaning the railing.

We did not meet the King of England during the ocean crossing to England. It was rumoured that he could be seen late at night, smoking strong cigarettes as he walked around the promenade deck, but late at night we were usually drinking and dancing. Admittedly there were very few women on board that beautiful ocean liner, but I was handsome and Mac was smooth and very funny, so our nights were full of excitement and adventure.

Our days were filled with mischief. Nowadays people are said to suffer from hyperactive attention deficit disorder or something like that. Well, we were hyperactive during the trip, and we caused a great deal of disorder and deficit because old Mac was the prince of practical jokes. We were never awake in time for breakfast, but at luncheon (as they called it) he would outline the plan for the day.

I was having the time of my life, and I believed that only goodness and positive success would be mine for the rest of it. I would be a war hero and come home to work on our family farm. Perhaps I would marry and have children, and in time teach them to fly and love the sky. At twenty years of age, drinking beer with the greatest friend I would ever have, I believed, I believed, I believed. Life was so wonderful.

Breakfast in Berlin

Five p.m., after the music lesson, found me sitting at the table in front of my breakfast of sausage and eggs. I was staring at the eight hooks and the three executioners when the condemned were shuffled into the chamber, positioned under their designated hook, hoisted up by two of the executioners, and suspended by a rope.

The camp commander, my music teacher, stood behind me with one hand on my shoulder. "Watch them die, Paine, and eat. Eat and you can go," he said.

I stared at the dying heroes and said no. Another fingernail was extracted and I was escorted back to my cell.

This scene would soon become commonplace, all part of the master plan to kill what was me and create something else. The pain where the fingernail had been torn away was awful, but I told myself that physical pain meant life and just might keep me from entering the dark side where monsters dwell, where the breakfast of eggs and sausage awaited.

Empress of Britain

Mac was missing a finger on his right hand, from a recent firecracker accident, he told me. On that first day he fashioned a fake finger, wrapped it in a large bandage and introduced himself to unsuspecting passengers and staff as John Hancock. He would shake hands and then pull back, and the victim would still have the finger. Mac would scream something like "Oh my god, the stitches didn't hold again!" or "Christ, man, let go sooner next time," and then run screaming down the hallway of the ship. My job was to watch and tell him later how well the joke had worked. It was so effective that some people ran after Mac with the fake pointer finger, screaming and apologizing.

The success of that little joke led to other, bigger and more potentially harmful pranks. There was the time, just before dinner, when we snuck into the first-class dining room. Paper cups were a fad in 1930s, described by the snooty as "containers with peripheral walls of rounded paper." The rich loved them because they could throw them away at their leisure. On that day we hid a large paper cup carefully between the water jug and the flower vase, upside down on the middle table for ten of that great room. Mac had made a jagged hole in the rim of the cup (which of course was then at the bottom) and added small scraps of paper littered about the table. In pen he wrote: *Danger! Do not lift this cup! Very dangerous poisonous spider underneath! It is a very small and white black widow. Run for your life if the spider escapes.*

At dinner that evening, it was not until dessert that the cup was noticed and the hysteria began. The room cleared within five minutes and it was reported that seven people had been bitten, all of them requiring a day or more in the Infirmary. A hunt for the arachnid was unsuccessful because of its colour, and the first-class dining room was fumigated with DDT.

It got better, because the spider joke was just a warmup. There was a passenger whom everyone disliked. He was one of those people who never stop talking and are an expert on everything. One evening he explained that devil worship and demonic possession were real. They required the correct words to clean things up and he had been instrumental in many successful exorcisms.

Mac turned to me and said, "He needs a lesson." A plan was hatched using an old Bible, candles and bedsheets. The first thing we did was memorize our lines from the black book, assuming the correct religious solemnity and posture. The second was to solicit the approval and participation of the man's roommate, and we were soon ready. At midnight the three of us approached the men's cabin and were ready to enter when the roommate informed us that he had left his key inside.

"No matter," declared my friend, and quietly opened the door with a lockpick. We donned our bedsheets with eyeholes and lit our candles. Then we surrounded the bed on which our victim was sleeping and began our chant: "*Exorcizamos te, omnis immunde spiritus, omnis satanica potestas, omnis infernalis adversarii, omnis legio, omnis congregatio et secta diabolica, in nomine et virtute Domini nostri Jesu Christi.*"

We were well into our third rendition and getting louder when the man woke up, screamed, and ran from the room, not to be seen again until disembarkation. Later his roommate was questioned by ship security, but he knew and had seen nothing, as he was drunk and on deck at the time of the demon exorcism. Mac and I were witnesses to the truth of his sworn statement.

Eventually we were caught, due to a prank that was perhaps a bit too much because it caused someone in the King's party to do something in his pants. We had stolen tomato sauce, a dozen eggs and a string of sausages from the kitchen. We then created two halves of a corpse, which we left bloody on the floor of the fourth-level elevator. The door opened and a man screamed and ran down the hallway, with the top half of the corpse chasing him. That was our final prank because Mac tripped on the sleeves of the stained shirt and fell at the feet of the ship's captain, who was just going to dinner.

We were confined to the ship's brig that night and brought before the captain and his officers in the morning. We were officially charged with mutiny on the high seas and for inciting unrest and fear among the crew and passengers of the ship — very serious charges, we were informed. Mac the lawyer started to speak and was told to shut up because a captain's word was the only law that mattered. We were quickly sentenced to death, with the execution to proceed forthwith.

Mac and I were cuffed and blindfolded and led outside, where we could hear a small crowd of angry people demanding our deaths. I was frightened and did not want to die. We were positioned somewhere near the edge of the promenade deck and our blindfolds were removed. In front of us a plank extended about six feet out from the ship. The captain declared that, according to an article of war or something, Mac and I would part company with the ship forever. He then instructed two of his crew to proceed with the execution.

When the crew member put his hand on my shoulder, I fully believed I was about to die. But I waited and waited, and then everybody started to laugh and whistle. We were released, suitably chastened, and allowed to proceed on our journey to England. "Gotcha," the captain said as he poured some single malt for each of us.

Mac and I disembarked that great ship as brothers, he to Scotland to be trained in something that he could not explain to me, and I to the Royal Air Force recruiting office in London.

"War is coming, brother," Mac said to me as he released

his hug. "I'm off to do my bit and you are off to do yours. And so we part."

I nodded to my friend and felt a darkness cover us both for a moment, like a fog from an evil place wanting to swallow our noble intentions. I felt drained after it moved on, and yelled to my friend as he was walking away, "Hey, MacDonald! Hey!"

He turned and I saw real fear on his face — a fear I had not expected, but I was certain that same foreboding and horror were reflected in my own.

"Brother, remember we will meet for a beer at that hotel you blathered on about, in one year plus one day, after the war ends. Bring your wife. The man with the most medals will pay. The Albion Hotel, right? Built by the son of Poseidon? Where Al Capone took his mistress?"

Mac waved his agreement and walked quickly away.

The gods Chaos and Fortuna are always laughing. They must have been screaming with glee that day.

Generals Without Trousers

Because I had travelled all the way from Pumpkin Town, Ontario, Canada, I was granted an interview with the Royal Air Force intake committee. Three heavily medalled overweight older gentlemen sat at a large table looking solemn and self-important. I was instructed by an under-ling to stand on an X, facing the scarred wooden table. From the colour and grain of the wood, the table looked like it had been constructed from a Canadian maple tree, so I was optimistic about my chances. As I waited, I began to think about maple syrup and pancakes and woodsmoke.

My thoughts were interrupted by one of the men seated before me. "Welcome, Gerald Kurt Paine, to the

Royal Air Force pilot-training admission process. You have travelled from Canada to request enrolment in our next cadre. Yes?"

I nodded curtly and said, "Yes, General, I would like to become a pilot and fight the Nazis in the war that is coming this way."

The officer shook his head sadly and said, "Young and uninformed Canadian, I am a wing commander in the Royal Air Force, not a general. Usually you will find creatures such as generals in the Army, floundering about in the mud. This is the Air Force. Do you, Mr. Paine, know what the Air Force does?"

"Yes, General — I mean, Wing Commander — I do."

The officer next to him asked, "And what is it that we do, Mr. Paine?"

I said, as quickly as I could, "At the present, World War I excepted, Wing Commander, you haven't done anything much. Sir, they are coming, and you will need men such as me. This is an island." My sarcastic answers have always had a saucy tone.

This second man stood, pointed to his uniform and said, "Do my insignia look like the Wing Commander's insignia?"

I looked as directed, and they were nothing alike. "Er, sorry, sir."

"I am in fact a group captain in the Royal Air Force," he informed me.

Big woopy shitballs, I thought to myself, and may have muttered the word "asshole."

The third man then took his turn attempting to destroy any self-confidence I might have had at the beginning of the interrogation. "Do not worry what rank I hold, Mr. Paine. It does not matter. What qualifications do you have? Do you bring any social connections or educational background from Ontario, Canada, that qualify you to enter our flight-training school?"

I told those pompous, anachronistic bastards about my first, unintended solo in 1936, and how afterwards I taught myself to fly the Curtiss Jenny that I had stolen. My background as a member of the farming community I glossed over quickly. I explained that I had completed Grade 13 with a 70 percent average and was qualified to attend university.

Sir Something Pompous stopped me then and asked, "You went to a school for the public, you say? A school for the masses? Public education?"

I nodded my reply, too angry with those assholes to speak.

"I have heard enough," one of them said. "Mr. Paine from Ontario, Canada, who claims to own a 1917 Curtiss Jenny, please go to the other room while we discuss your application. Do not bother sitting down, as we will not take long, I assure you."

I went to the other room and sat on a chair facing away from the door. A minute later, as I was gazing at the front page of a London newspaper, I was called back into the torture chamber. The newspaper had a black-and-white picture of somebody important; he looked a bit like Bertie, whom I had met on the train from Toronto. The man in the picture was waving at a large crowd as he disembarked from a large ship. He looked distinctly unhappy.

I found the X, moved three paces forward, and stared at the three judges with full-force Canadian anger.

The general in the middle rearranged and then flattened some official-looking papers, then raised his red-rimmed eyes to mine. "Paine, old chap, you are just not one of us. You lack the good breeding and manners that are demanded of those who fly our aircraft. We see ourselves

as knights of the air, while you are more of a peasant —
a tiller of the soil, if you will. Thank you for coming all
this way from the colonies to see us. Perhaps the Canadian
Army would be a more appropriate match for you. Hard
cheese, old chap. Good day to you, sir."

I was ushered to the door by an underling who rolled
his eyes towards the three men who had just destroyed the
hopes and dreams of a determined and able young man.
Just then I remembered the letter Bertie had given me. He
had shaken my hand firmly when we parted in Montreal
and told me to give the letter to any pompous asshole at
the War Office or flight school who seemed "all mouth and
no trousers." I was certain this was the exact situation that
my friend Bertie had been talking about.

I carefully removed the letter from my back pocket
and for the first time noticed an orange seal that looked
like a pumpkin embedded neatly in the wax. The three
generals at the table seemed to recognize the seal right off.
The general on the right got up from behind the table and
asked to see the letter. He broke the seal and read it aloud,
as if he was being forced to eat shit.

June 2, 1939
Montreal, Canada

To whom it may concern:

*Before you stands my friend Gerald Kurt Paine, a
Canadian, and one loyal to the Commonwealth. He is,
in my opinion as your King, exactly the kind of man
the Royal Air Force and England will require in the
dreaded days ahead. Gerald Paine has my confidence and
my full support.*

*Please give Pilot Candidate Paine my very best regards
and best wishes as he pursues his dream.
George R.*

Each of us in that room were dumbfounded by the contents of the letter. I had ridden the rails as a stowaway with the King of England, and he was my friend. It had been his image that I had seen on the front page of the newspaper.

I began my pilot training the next day.

Hands-On Kind of Guy

Thanks to the King of England and not my stellar performance while pleading my case in front of the selection committee, I was to become a fighter pilot. It did not occur to me that I could fail at such a thing. After all, I had taught myself to fly a Curtiss Jenny with no formal instruction of any kind and had dropped rotten pumpkins on city streets while flying upside down.

Ground school, which is another name for classroom learning, almost grounded me forever. I had lied when I told the generals I had a 70 percent average in my final year of high school in Ontario and had qualified to attend university. I was more of a hands-on learner who did well when building or taking apart something like a car, a tractor or an airplane. Ground school found me sitting at a desk, listening and taking notes, plus memorizing and applying the stuff we were taught. Worst of all, I quickly discovered that mathematics and science are a big part of flying. I had to calculate this and that and extrapolate this to that. There were graphs and charts and things like windspeed versus airspeed and various rotation speeds. Then there was the science, full of ideas like Bernoulli's Law and Newton's motion ideas, density altitude, climate and weather, among other things.

Understanding navigation was a nightmare. The difference between true north and magnetic north and compass deviation still elude me. Did you know that magnetic north changes over time? Did you know that the shortest route from Labrador to London is a circle? At home, Jenny and I just flew in a straight line from the farm to the town and back or followed the country roads. The ground-school teachers made flying very complicated for me.

Except for the tiny section on airframes and engines, I failed the ground-school examinations and found myself before another group of Royal Air Force generals. I noticed that the letter the King had given me on the train to Montreal had been placed on top of my examination papers. There was a lot of red ink on those papers. The conversation went something like this:

"Ah, Royal Air Force Pilot Cadet Paine, you seemed to have forgotten to answer the questions correctly. I am sure it was an oversight on your part. Is that correct, Mr. Paine?"

"Actually, sir — "

"Shut up, Paine," the man said very calmly.

"Shutting up here, Wing Commander. Shutting up, sir. Sorry, sir."

"No harm done, no harm done. It happens sometimes that cadets do not bring their thinking caps to the examinations. Is that what happened this time, Paine?"

"I — "

"I told you to shut up, Paine."

I did not say a word. I was wondering if a thinking cap was something people wore for tests.

The Wing Commander stood up and reached for two items that had been lurking behind him. The first, a very large metal globe of the earth, he threw at me with a very strange, almost straight-arm, over-the-head pitch. I caught the globe by letting it hit me in the chest and then wrapping my arms around it. I had played football in school, and it was the sort of catch a punt receiver would make.

The Wing Commander turned to his colleagues and said, "Son of a bitch was paying attention, and that is good. And his reflexes are fine."

The others did not laugh, because they knew that if I had not caught the globe, I would have been gone from the Royal Air Force academy. It had been a very real test.

I was handed a long piece of string. A young pilot sitting behind me, whom I had not noticed upon entering that chilly room, said, "Cadet Paine, you seem quite unable — pardon me, without your thinking cap you seem quite unable to grasp certain, shall we say, basic concepts. You will have noticed that on the globe, Toronto, your capital city, and London, our capital city, have been marked with white chalk. Now, using the string, find the shortest route from your capital city to ours. You have exactly one minute by my watch. Now begin."

I placed one end of the string on Ottawa, the capital city of Canada, and the other end on London, the capital city of England, and tied a knot to show the distance. Then I did nothing for a few seconds, until it came to me in a flash, like the ideas and insights that occurred to me sometimes when I was working on a broken piece of farm machinery or had a problem with the corn. I placed the bitter end of the string on Ottawa again and made an arc up towards the north and then down to London. The string was shorter this time — much shorter — and I knew why. The answer was obvious: I had demonstrated the principal of the great circle.

The Flight Lieutenant said, "Time's up. Well done, Cadet Paine. We had hoped you could do it. Well done, indeed. You indeed own a thinking cap."

The Wing Commander said, "Well, he's not stupid, just dumb. We will keep dumb, because the dumb can learn. The stupid cannot learn, as we well know." The others smiled this time; it seemed an old joke.

The officer to the right of the Wing Commander spoke then. By then it was obvious to me that he was not a wing commander but an air chief marshal. "Mr. Paine, I have a friend, the captain of the *Empress of Britain*, and he told me a story about two dumb young men who almost walked the plank into the Atlantic Ocean. He mentioned something about poisonous spiders and ghosts. We in the Royal Air Force also have a plank, and it leads to the infantry. Our plank is reserved for stupid cadets and for cadets who forget to put on their thinking caps. Are you stupid, sir? If we let you continue with your pilot training, will you remember to wear your thinking helmet at all times?"

I did not speak or move. It was not a question that I dared answer, for fear of the many traps inherent in it. Instead I willed myself not to look too stupid and not to blink as I stared at the highest-ranking member of the Royal Air Force, Hugh Dowding.

"We are going to give you a chance to locate said cap and then pass the examinations. Furthermore, we will provide you some assistance with your search." Air Chief Marshal Dowding pointed to the flying officer who had asked the question about the globe and who was again sitting in the chair in the back corner by the window. He had been staring at the clouds and watching a small aircraft landing and taking off in one beautiful movement. "This is Flying Officer Smith. He, like you, once upon a dumb time forgot his thinking cap, and he will now help you find yours."

I was told that I was going to repeat the entire ground

school, minus the engine portion, and pass or be sent to the Army — via a wooden plank — for basic training. Then they handed me a letter with another orange pumpkin seal. The letter read simply, *Everyone needs a friend.* It was signed *Bertie.*

I did not impress anyone on the second go-round, but with extra help from my instructor and that letter signed by the head of England as motivation, I passed the written examinations. As I was struggling with the math questions, an old-timer walked by as I was working on some calculations. He stopped, had a look at my work and then cleared his throat loudly. I redid the math and he moved on.

Classroom work took place at the same time as we were learning to fly the de Havilland Tiger Moth. You are probably thinking what I was thinking as I approached the little airplane for my first lesson. I owned and could fly a Curtiss Jenny, and the two planes looked alike. I expected to master the Moth quickly and be on my way to bigger aircraft, and I was correct.

As I've explained before, I was a hands-on man. Most cadets flew on their own after five to ten hours of instruction, but I took only two hours to solo. Stalls, spins, steep turns and inverted flight were fun and exciting, and my instructors were very happy with my progress. They said I was a natural and passed me on to advanced training. It was all so perfect. I remember the ease of movement and the peace of mind as I learned newer and more complicated manoeuvres.

During advanced training we were introduced to the much more powerful North American Harvard. As I learned to fly this larger airplane, the classroom-based lessons continued in various subjects. I paid attention this time and discovered that I was not as dumb as I had first thought. I passed both the written examination for advanced flight training and the flight examination and received my pilot's wings. I had racked up two hundred flying hours in total.

The names of our graduating class were posted in the *London Gazette* and we each received a piece of paper signed by the King. Mine said:

> George VI, by the Grace of God, of Great Britain, Ireland and the British Dominions beyond the Seas, King, Defender of the Faith, Emperor of India, etc. To Our Trusty and well-beloved *Gerald Kurt Paine*, Greeting:
> We, reposing especial Trust and Confidence in your Loyalty, Courage, and Good conduct, do by these Presents Constitute and Appoint you to be an Officer in Our *Royal Air Force* from the *First* day of *April* 1940.

I was a pilot officer in the Royal Air Force. My friend Bertie, King of Almost Everywhere, said so, and I was thrilled. A farm boy from rural Ontario, Canada, had stolen and hitched rides to England and, with good luck and a bit of skill, had become a pilot officer in the Royal Air Force.

Next was operational training, where I learned to fly a Hurricane, the larger cousin of the Spitfire. The training for frontline duties was a bit rushed because they needed pilots ready and able to fight the German air force massing in Europe. It was early April 1940 and the war had been on since September 1, 1939.

In those days, fighter aircraft such as the Spitfire and Hurricane were called "crates" and I was called a "sprog" or "child" — impulsive and stupid — because I was new and struggling to keep up with the speed and complexity of those beasts. I remember being lined up on the runway and ready to go like it was yesterday. Out loud I would recite:

> Mixture is rich.
> Both mags are on, checked and within range.
> Primer is locked.
> Propeller is fully forward.
> Fuel on, main tanks; booster pump on.
> Flaps at clean.
> Gauges all working.
> Gyros set to the compass.
> Harness is secure.
> Canopy closed and locked.
> Review emergency procedures for engine failure after takeoff: 95 knots for glide speed and clean; 85 knots, flaps down.
> Plus-four pounds of boost and off we go.
> Gear up before the 103 knots gear-limiting speed, which will happen damn fast with 1,200 horses in front pulling us along.
> Power back to climb: 2,400 rpm and plus-four pounds.

And then I was flying the great beast.

My Jenny, when she was in a good mood, might do eighty miles per hour. The Hurricane would stall and fall from the sky at around sixty miles per hour. Then there was the matter of sheer power. My Jenny had ninety horses pulling her along, while the Hurricane had around 1,200 horsepower, or as they explained in class, two horsepower per pound (whatever that meant). It could go like stink, which was my real issue.

My Jenny was slow and flew along at about eighty miles per hour, as I've said. This gave me plenty of time to think and plan as we dawdled along above the countryside, navigating and looking at stuff. The Hurricane was nick-named "Hurry" by everyone; I do not know the origin of the name, but it was always "Hurry does this" and "darling Hurry can do that." What I knew was that sweet Hurry could fly at 350 miles per hour straight and level, give or take. At first, I could not think fast enough to keep up with the demands of darling Hurry, to fulfill the needs of my powerful and sexy aircraft, but that was everyone's struggle at first. Then came the day when I climbed into my Hurry and it was easy. *Easy* led to *skillful*, and by early May 1940 I was ready to meet the Hun.

It was with trepidation that I joined my fighter squadron near the west coast of France. Like everyone else, I was certain that I would be killed with the first wave of enemy fighters. I was still a sprog, so the squadron leader wisely positioned me at the rear of our formation, my main duty being to guard the tails of those at the front. Then we practised and practised, waited and waited, and drank Burton ale by the barrel.

Stuka

It was late May 1940 when Dunkirk happened. We were briefly stationed in France prior to the horror on those beaches. We were low on spare parts, ammunition, fuel and a positive attitude. The war was going badly and we, the Royal Air Force, were doing little to help the troops retreating across France towards that beach as they trea-sured a forlorn hope of escape across the Channel to England. I and the others in our group had been ordered to avoid enemy contact and proceed across the Channel to preserve and repair our Hurricanes. I took off later than the others because I had pretended to have a mechanical difficulty. I wanted to make a detour to the beach to have a look.

I heard before I saw the two German Stuka bombers, killing machines that the Polish people had first encountered in 1939. They were diving and killing the British troops lined up on the beach, waiting to board tiny boats that might take them home to a hot cup of tea and perhaps some toast and jam.

The Stuka was a scary thing, especially for the unprotected troops. It was a two-man fighter bomber with a hellish siren that the pilot turned on as he made his killing run. Hollywood later used that sound for any airplane on a bombing run, and that still angers me. I'm sure that you know the sound.

My first two kills as a Royal Air Force fighter pilot were those Stuka fighter bombers. The siren increased in volume and frequency as the Stuka approached the men on the ground, but I knew that the little propeller that generated the sound, located under the fuselage, also slowed down an aircraft that was already very slow and could not outrun me. I'm not certain, but as I chased the dive-bombers inland from the beach it seemed like I was at least a hundred miles per hour faster. I quickly shot the left wing from the nearest aircraft and watched it enter a crazy spin that caused the siren to sputter and shriek. As I killed the pilot of the second Stuka, I added my own words to the famous lines that I had been forced to memorize in school: "Out, out, brief candle, you son of a bitch! Life's but a walking shadow, a poor player, and your plane that struts and frets with stupid sirens along the beach is slow and then is heard no more. It is a tale told by a Nazi idiot, full of sound and fury, signifying nothing."

Afterwards I did a barrel roll at full throttle, two hundred feet above our brave troops along the beach, wishing them luck on their journey home. Because I was out of ammunition, I headed across the Channel as ordered to prepare for the inevitable battle for Britain. As I made my way over the water, I realized that courage is simply putting fear into a box, locking that box and hiding the key somewhere near your testicles. I did another barrel roll as I laughed.

Generally, in those days, when a pilot shot down an enemy aircraft and nobody saw it happen, it did not count as a kill. I was prepared for that eventuality as I flew to our new airfield. Upon landing I was told to report to our commanding officer. He congratulated me for ridding the world of two screaming Nazi bastard dive-bombers — someone had seen and reported what had happened. Then my CO confined me to barracks for one hour, for disobeying orders. The hour was to give my mates a head start with the women in town.

All Nine Yards

August 13, 1940, was the day Adolf Hitler proclaimed that his penis was bigger than Winston Churchill's. To prove it, he ordered his airplanes to beat up our airplanes and gave the job to a fat bastard named Goering. *Fair enough*, we thought as we sat in chairs in the bright sunshine outside our squadron office, drinking tea and falling asleep, expecting nothing to happen because we had been on watch since the middle of July. We talked about going to town for a Burton after supper and perhaps catching a show. There was a young woman I had been paying attention to and thought I might give her a ring. I was reading a *Farmer's Almanac* that my dad had sent and was thinking about the farm and wondering how many rows of corn he had planted.

The phone rang. We jumped to our feet and listened to the dispatch officer speak with an unknown at the other end. It was a wrong number, so we settled back into idle conversation. I was thinking about pumpkins, corn, women I had known, the fall fair and, of course, that woman I wanted to know better. The phone rang again, and it seemed more urgent this time. It was Operations, sending orders to intercept a large formation of enemy bombers and fighters crossing the Channel towards southern England and our airfields.

This was it at last — the enemy were on their way. As we prepared to run to our waiting Hurricanes, our commander stopped us for one of his chats. He said, very slowly and calmly, "Remember, we fly to the target in three groups of four — finger-four formation, the Royal Air Force ideas be damned. When I give the order, dive among the bastards and forget everything except *kill*. Just dive and kill; there will be no quarter given and you will show no mercy. They are here to kill you and your loved ones and to turn our country into a Nazi state. Now, my fine fellows, go!"

Then he stumped over to his Hurricane, which was conveniently parked beside our squad room. This man would become famous later as a great leader and a fearless pilot. He would survive the war as a prisoner of war in Germany.

We had the sun behind us and about a hundred enemy bombers with 109s escorting them into England below and to the right. I was in my designated place at the back of the squadron when a strange calm descended over my mind and body and I felt happy and content. It was the same feeling I had after the drunk pilot fell from his Jenny and I decided to live. The propeller of my Hurricane seemed to slow and bend and the chatter on the radio became distorted and almost too slow to comprehend. The command to attack from our famous English leader seemed slurred, as if coming from an intoxicated man, but I understood what he wanted of us, the Horsemen of the Apocalypse, the Twelve Paladins of Charlemagne. I believed that I had been born for that day, for those times, and that as the enemy attempted to penetrate England with their ugly cross, I and my mates, the British bulldogs of war, would stop them. And so, as I descended among the enemy, I felt no fear, only calm and a heightened awareness of time and the three dimensions of space.

The heavy bombers twisted and turned out of our way and the dark ME 109s darted like swallows as they attempted to defend their colleagues. Two of the MEs saw that I was zeroing in on a Dornier that was slowly turning to avoid our attack. The fighters came at me from the side. I abandoned my pursuit of the bomber and made the tightest turn my Hurricane could manage, almost falling into an uncontrolled spin — almost, but not quite. Neither German fighter could stay with me during that curve, so within a few seconds I was sitting behind both aircraft, one to my left and one to the right and slightly higher.

One fighter was beginning to draw away from me, so I turned towards him, aimed quickly with the reflector gunsight, turned the nose of my Hurricane slightly ahead of the dot, and sent a short burst to where I knew the Messerschmidt would soon be. I watched as the German aircraft flew into the spray of bullets and then disintegrated. Back home I knew how to lead a rabbit before I shot it. They called it "deflection shooting" at fighter training, and I was very good at it.

The second fighter was now making a tight turn to his left, and that was a mistake. I turned with him and shot off the upper portion of the starboard wing. He and his friend in the other 109 tumbled to the ground and I moved on, looking for a bomber to take out of commission. I knew where they would be, so I reduced my throttle, inverted my Hurry, sent a quick thank-you to the drunk who had first demonstrated this manoeuvre (and to Jenny, of course) and dove straight down to where two German Junkers 88s were trying to make it further inland towards our airfields. I raked the closest once across the cockpit, and I'm certain that I killed both pilots.

Our Hurricanes had only about ten to twelve seconds of fire, and by then all four 20 mm Oerlikon cannons were empty. So, I flew behind the second 88 and gently destroyed its rudder with my propeller. I have no idea what happened to that Junkers, but it is very difficult to steer and land an airplane of that size without a working rudder. I retrieved my pocketknife from the top pocket of my flight suit and carved four inch-long notches on the top of my instrument panel, just above the airspeed indicator.

We flew five sorties that day, but after that initial encounter I had no further kills to my credit. A couple of perhaps or maybes, but the two bombers that I hit seemed undamaged. They quickly released their cargo over Nowhere, England, turned about and headed back to Germany, their job undone. Again, my ammunition was gone, but I watched them briefly as they flew eastward.

At the end of the day, I inspected my crate and quickly realized how tough a Hawker Hurricane could be. The propeller had large nicks and scrapes and, to my surprise, bullet holes riddled most of the fuselage along both sides. One of the maintenance crew pointed to the starboard wing, which had bits and pieces missing near the aileron.

Back home when something or someone was referred to as a "brick shithouse," it meant it or they were a bit ugly but tough, durable and unstoppable. I decided, therefore, to name my aircraft the *Brick Shithouse*. A few days later, when I had a few minutes between sorties, I stole some orange and black paint from the maintenance shack and painted four pumpkins squishing four swastikas at the back of the fuselage near the tail. I printed the new nickname in red, next to the cowling. It was perfect. Brick shithouse indeed — a bit ugly, but tough.

Hubris

Many fighter pilots battling the enemy over England and the Channel during the Battle of Britain suffered from hubris. We who survived the initial encounters with the enemy pilots became arrogant and somewhat foolish in our behaviour and attitude. As you know, first comes the pride and then the fall. I'm trying to remember the name of that Greek guy with wings made from wax. His dad was Daedalus, I think. The kid's name was Icier something. Anyway, he thought he knew it all — until the sun melted the wax and he went kaput, just like me.

I returned late one afternoon with a bullet-riddled Hurry, having shot down two heavy bombers. In the briefing room I was told that they would be counted as probable kills but not confirmed kills. I had seen them smash into the ground as I flew overhead at five thousand feet, but nobody else had seen it happen. The pride of hubris indeed. I was angry and hurt and cared only about the numbers and tallies on the chart at the front of the briefing room. I cared only for my kill count, because I wanted to be the most famous pilot of all.

If you have been following my story carefully you will ask this question: If I was an ace fighter pilot, why has nobody today heard of my exploits? There are no written records of those weeks. Why? It is because of what I did during those terrible days, what a stupid, young, eager, passionate boy-man did on one of our sorties, intent on his wax wings. It turned me into a ghost that lives in a box and is forced to wear goggles and an old steel helmet.

We pilots talked quite a bit about how the ME 109 was faster than a Hurricane but perhaps not quite as quick as a Spitfire. By then we also knew, from experience in combat, that our Hurries could turn on a shilling and that we were better — or perhaps more desperate — pilots. I think desperation is a better way to explain our success, because fighting to survive is different from fighting to conquer.

Looking upwards from the ground, a dogfight seemed fast and complicated, with vapour trails everywhere. The only way to distinguish the enemy aircraft from our own was by looking for the distinctive colouring of the wings of the Spitfires and Hurricanes: on the underside, the wing on the left was black and the one on the right was white. When you were up there in the mix, everyone was moving at about the same speed, and it all seemed so slow. Einstein called this relativity, and he had the right of it.

The ME 109 in front of me and below was moving away from me very slowly, relative to the speed of the Hurricane. I knew that I could get that Messerschmidt because I was above and therefore had gravity working for me. I dove towards that German fighter, who was so intent on guarding the German bombers that he did not see me until I had sent a quick burst slightly ahead of his propeller, so that he flew directly into a fast-moving cascade of cannon fire. I was getting very good at that kind of killing.

The ME 109 with a dead pilot spiralled to the ground and crashed onto a field somewhere in southern England.

Most important to me was that another Hurricane pilot had witnessed the crash and would confirm that kill. *Good*, I thought to myself, but I wanted more. I knew that a Henkel heavy bomber was above me and to the west. Full throttle and nose up, a slight left aileron and left rudder, and the bomber was in my sights. I shot off the tail and down it went in an uncontrolled spiral dive. This time there were no Royal Air Force pilots nearby to confirm what had happened, so I followed that crippled bomber all the way to the ground, shooting it with everything I had left. Nobody escaped — my cannon fire killed the crew as they tried to bail out. It would be a confirmed kill because I knew precisely where to find the wreckage. I was overjoyed.

I rejoined my squadron and we returned to our airfield to be refuelled and rearmed. We had a quick cup of tea and then again joined the melees in the blue sky above England. I shot down another fighter before the day was over, and that gave me seven kills in a matter of weeks.

I was officially a fighter pilot ace, and that was what I wanted to be. By the end of the weeks of intense air combat that has been called the Battle of Britain, I had thirteen kills to my credit. Only a few others such as Bader and Johnson had more kills to their credit at that point. I was a cocky idiot by then, with that waxy hubris I was telling you about.

Under a Bridge

Dreams and nightmares are the same thing for me, and the topic of those subconscious endeavours is always the same. Sometimes I am shooting that Henkel bomber as it descends towards its destruction. Other times I am a fellow pilot who, later in the squadron hut, confirms that episode as a kill but then turns to me and sneers, *A bit of overkill, old chap. A bit over the top on that one, wouldn't you say?* On rare occasions I am the German bomber pilot screaming for his father as he burns and then bleeds when the bullets from my cannon fire penetrate his body and the bodies of his crew.

When I awaken from my dreams, I am always the monster — hungry and nasty.

London

Churchill was either a genius or a crazy loon. The attacks on British airfields, if allowed to continue, would have won the Battle of Britain for our enemy. I witnessed the effects of those attacks every day. Every day a little more had been done to destroy our ability to maintain and use our Spits and Hurricanes. Something had to be done, and Churchill did it.

Goering had bragged weeks earlier that Berlin would never be bombed by the Royal Air Force. On August 25, 1940, a force of seventy British aircraft bombed Berlin. I and others were flying escort that day and witnessed it all. The German anti-aircraft fire was so intense that most of the bombers missed their intended targets, but the point was that Goering and his boss were being delivered a message that we were very much alive, willing and able to deliver a mighty blow to the very centre of Germany. Of course, that was true, but the real reason we had been sent was to anger the Führer so much that he would have a Nazi tantrum and then retaliate by bombing London rather than the airfields. This seemingly insignificant gesture, by a fat Englishman with a cigar stuck between his teeth who had very large testicles in his trousers, changed everything.

By September fifteenth we were soul-tired but determined to continue right to the end. On that day we ate bacon and eggs before sunrise and then sat in our usual spots on the turf outside the squadron hut. I was reading the well-worn almanac when the telephone rang, a little later that normal that day.

We had been fighting since the middle of August to protect our airfields. The German bombers, we were told, were now heading for London. I thought about my friend Bertie and his family as I strapped myself and my parachute into the cockpit of my weathered Hurricane and prepared to defend the capital city of England.

September was a long month, and so was October. Watching a city burn from above is tough, but London took it on the chin, the airfields were repaired, and we had some time to get our crates into tiptop shape. The sacrifice of the people of London saved England.

Down

October twenty-seventh had been a very busy day for Royal Air Force Pilots. I was twenty-two years old and had just survived a horrific air battle off the coast of England near the Channel. Sword rage still pumped through my veins and into my heart — I wanted to kill and then kill again. I chased a damaged twin-engine Messerschmitt Bf 110 across the water without waiting to be told not to leave England. I had reached the coast of France and the 110 was in my sights before I realized that another Messerschmitt, a 109, was on my tail and firing. Too late I inverted my Hurry and dove for the ground, turned sharply to the left, then right and finally made a tight climbing turn to the left. Unfortunately, I stalled my aircraft and it began to spin towards France, out of control.

I felt bullets strike my engine and watched as smoke and flames erupted in front of the fire wall. My beautiful Hurry was doomed — the German bullets had done their worst. The prop was windmilling on its own, bereft of power; the controls were stiff but working. It was getting dark and the ground below was invisible, so a forced landing was out of the question. It didn't matter anyway, because we had been instructed over and over never to leave the enemy a whole aircraft. I opened the canopy, inverted the Hurry, undid my harness and, like my first flying instructor, fell towards the ground. I counted to five and opened the parachute, hoping it would work.

I remember laughing as I fell towards occupied France. I was the ultimate adrenaline junkie long before the term was invented. All of us who flew fighters during the war were addicted to excitement and danger and, of course, Burton's ale. As I floated in the darkness, I thought about the conversation that would happen in the barracks when it was reported that I was missing, presumed killed.

"Where's our man gone, then?"

"Oh, Paine you're referring to? Well, he's gone for a Burton." Rather than admit that a friend, a comrade, had been killed, we would pretend that the missing man was at the pub — and it worked. It was our slanguage, designed to help us not think too much.

I had gone for a Burton for sure. The trees managed to miss me when I landed and there was little jarring. Scrambling to gather my parachute, I heard the noises of the enemy searching. I hid my chute, ran past some trees, picked a tall tree, climbed to the top, made a little nest, got comfortable and fell asleep. All the pilots fighting the German Luftwaffe during the battle for Britain in 1940 had learned to fall asleep in seconds.

France

I awoke as daylight gave some incipient warmth to the day. I urinated in every direction up in that tree, trying to avoid a cascade of urine going from branch to branch and then to the ground. Then I listened and heard all the natural noises, coming to me one at a time. First the crickets, then the singing of larks in the meadow, and finally the wind making its way through the branches and over the hay fields, newly harvested, the large stacks ready for the barn. I deemed it safe to climb down and then wander aimlessly, hoping for something good to happen.

On the ground I opened a pocket in my flight suit and ate some chocolate. I was congratulating myself for my cunning when a voice said, "*L'homme du Christ, nous avons cherché toute la nuit pour vous. Nous ne t'aurions jamais trouvé si tu n'avais pas pissé sur l'arbre.*"

"Parley only a little *petit* Francis," I said. I spoke fluent German, but it seemed like a bad idea to tell them that until later.

Another voice, a woman: "My friend said that you are an idiot for pissing down the tree. That's how we finally found you. Did you not know that piss stinks? The Krauts are everywhere. We have to move."

"Who are you?" I asked the voices. Three men and a woman emerged, armed with tommy guns.

"*La Résistance*, here to help you live a little bit longer, perhaps. We saw the plane crash and saw you bail out. It is fortunate that the Krauts are stupid and lazy. The treehouse was good yes but pissing from the top was a bad idea." She pointed to the urine stains on the trunk and pretended to sniff. "Your next tree fort would have been in heaven."

The men chuckled very quietly when she translated into French what she had said. "But first we leave this maple and hide over there until they pass us by." The woman with the large gun pointed to the tanks and infantry now moving down the road towards us. I had not seen them or heard them.

We dashed across the open field and into a haystack that was not an ordinary stack of hay. The hay was piled over a small door that led underground to a small room. In it was water and food and, of course, my friend John MacDonald, clutching a radio.

Mac was grinning like he had just seduced the prom queen. He had an open bottle of red wine in his hand. "Hey, old chap," he said, and hugged me and kissed me on both cheeks. "Gary, these French spies know how to spy in comfort. Who would've thought to build a room under a haystack and stock it with booze? *Stock* it. Get it?"

The woman motioned for us to be quiet and whispered, "*Putain d'idiot.*" It was then that I heard a tank and troops almost upon us.

We listened as the tank rolled noisily towards our hiding room underground. MacDonald had chosen to sit beside our female partisan and she beside him, and they were holding hands. I was not certain if that was wise, considering the kind of work they had chosen. The heavy machine rolled on and over our haystack and then was gone. Next came the German infantry, and they soon had also moved on. We opened another bottle of wine, finished it and then peered cautiously from our hole in the ground.

An outlier, not paying much attention or seeming to care about the day's agenda, was sauntering towards us, kicking stones and softly whistling a tune I recognized and would get to know better at another place and another time. When the man passed near our position, the partisans leapt forward, quickly stuffed dirty rags into his mouth and dragged him, arms flailing wildly, back into our chamber. I was reminded of wolf spiders I had watched in the barn at our farm as they pounced on unsuspecting bugs. The man's helmet was quickly removed, another piece of cloth was stuffed into his mouth, and his arms were pinioned to his sides with barbed wire. It was difficult to tell the man's age in the dark, but later, with a bit of gentle persuasion, he admitted to being nineteen years old and newly arrived in France from his home in Munich. He explained that he had been behind the others because he had stopped to urinate and was trying to catch up.

We waited an hour and then we, the wolf spiders, dragged our unfortunate captive to an abandoned farm. More than once I was shown how to walk without stepping on twigs and tripping. I noticed that the woman and Mac accidentally touched on occasion. Our captive was half carried and half dragged along the path with the friendly support of the other French Resistance soldiers.

As he walked, I saw that Mac was attached to two things. The first was a compact radio transceiver and the second was the beautiful partisan woman. She reminded me of a ferocious wild animal, a predator. Her automatic weapon was slung over her right shoulder with the dangerous end pointing to wherever she was looking. Occasionally this spine-chilling paladin grasped the handle of a small knife that was tucked into her leather belt. She saw me staring at her blade, pulled it out, grabbed Mac by his pudenda and mimicked castrating him. "*Monsieur* pilot, it is the knife for cutting balls from a pig. You understand this?" she asked in English. I nodded and she smiled.

"What she meant, old chum, is that she cuts the twin generals from any German soldier she captures, before she cuts his throat," Mac explained helpfully as he smoothed his pants.

"Christ" was all I said. I was beginning to understand that the war on the ground was a very personal affair and more brutal than anything I had done so far. Shooting at another fighter aircraft from a distance, hidden inside a warm cockpit, was clean and impersonal, almost a game. I had never witnessed blood pouring from a dying man's crotch — at least, not to that point.

Mac wasn't finished. He said, "The Germans have a name for her. Lorraine is the *Schneider Frau.* After slicing the balls off, she nails the bloody things to the nearest post or wall, with a note attached that reads something along the lines of '*Ein weniger Vater für das Vaterland.*'" Mac kissed the woman passionately. I finally understood that this beautiful, magnificent French patriot was his wife.

"So, you're an iffy-umpty, then?" I looked at the radio my friend was carrying. "And this lady, of course, is your wife?"

"Yes to both. I first trained in Whitby, Ontario. You know where Whitby is, I assume. From my training in Whitby (Oshawa really) I travelled to England on that ship where you almost had us sleeping with the sharks and jellyfish. Final training was in the Highlands of Scotland. I've been in France, assisting these people, for a few months." Mac held up his shortened finger, laughed and added, "I am an explosives expert too. The irony, my friend, is that I could not join the Canadian Army because of high blood pressure. They said the stress would kill me."

At the farm we turned our attention to the boy we had captured. We removed the gag that was choking him. The soldier did not speak French or English, but with my excellent German I was the translator that afternoon. The man was stripped of his uniform and underclothing and was tied to a stained wooden post with more cruel wire.

The wire was tight and drew copious amounts of blood from his wrists, ankles and neck. The German begged me to plead for his life with the *verrückte verdammte Partisanen* because he was not a Nazi, hated Hitler and was in the army because he had been impelled by his father to join the *Armee* as soon as he turned eighteen. He had never hurt anyone and just wanted to live and see his family again.

I did not reply because I was not in charge. I was merely a pilot who had been stupid enough to chase a Messerschmidt 110 across the Channel and then be shot down in occupied France in October 1940. I told him as much, and he hung his head and was quiet.

Lorraine had been looking at Mac and stroking his cheek while the German begged for his life. She turned and looked at me to make sure I translated what she said. She kissed Mac with more tenderness and love than I had ever seen and smiled. Then she grasped the young German by his dangling testicles, squeezed hard and said, "Be clear about this, vermin, we do not need information from you. You will die today very painfully. All I need from you is your pain and some Master Race suffering. I want to hear your screams."

"Please, I am a good man. I have hurt nobody. Please!" the man screamed at the partisan.

Lorraine pointed at my friend MacDonald and said to me, "Tell this bastard about to die that I am a married woman, married to that man — that man with the radio, the Canadian. We had a child together and now she is dead. She was just a child, a child crying in my arms, when they took her and threw her against a wall and smeared her brains all over the yellow bricks of our yard. She was beautiful and innocent and loving and oh, so sweet."

MacDonald looked at his wife and she at him. He fell

to his knees and held her to him. She stroked Mac's hair gently and then looked at the hapless boy hanging from the post. Mac's wife stepped over to the German. She squeezed his balls, pulled them towards her, and turned her gelding knife in their direction. We left that place an hour later.

Partisans are Insane

Life with the French underground was thrilling and bloody terrifying. I worked with them until I decided I had had enough. The partisans were brave and ruthless and knew that capture meant extreme torture and execution. Some of those brave people were constantly morose and quiet, while others used humour and good cheer to get through the fear and horror of their work. Mac was one of the latter and his lovely wife was one of the former. His jokes were stupid and were known as "whisper jokes"; they always drew a groan or yowl and made everyone relax for a few minutes. His wife, our leader, was quick to bring everyone back into focus on the task at hand. They were a fantastic pair of resistance fighters.

One such joke was delivered just before entering a small village to place anti-Nazi posters on walls and posts. Mac turned to me and asked in French and then English, "Gary, which of the Peters makes the most noise?" He pointed to one of the partisans, who was named Pierre. Pierre, a burly Frenchman, had been a hunter before the war and knew how to move in silence. He looked at Mac as if he had lost his mind.

I answered, "No idea."

His wife whispered, "Shut up, MacDonald. You are a fucking loud stupid Canadian asshole."

Mac laughed and said, "The trumpeter, of course."

Mac wasn't finished. He loved puns above all else. "Hey, why is Peter Pan always flying? Anyone? Gary? No? Because he *never lands*. Get it? That was a Peter Pun joke. It never grows old. I know that one was tear-able. You want another one?"

Pierre, who spoke very little, whispered, "No more stupid English jokes, radio man."

MacDonald turned to Pierre and said, "Okay. Because you ask, I will tell one more at our next stop."

Before the execution of a family of traitors who had given valuable information to the Nazis, just before they were hung, Mac laughed and then asked his wife, "Dear, how many traitors does it take to change a lightbulb?" She told him to hush. His answer was "Three. Do you know why, my dear?"

"Shut the fuck up, John MacDonald. This is serious. These three pieces of *merde* are about to die and I'm certain they see no humour in what you are saying. Canadians are so ill-mannered!"

"Okay, I see that none of you get it, so I will tell you. The answer is three, of course. One to get a table, stand on it and screw in the bulb, and two to tell the Nazis about it." The punchline delivered, each of the informers was pushed off the table on which they had been standing (bullets to the head would have made too much noise). We all snickered as we finally understood the stupid joke.

The traitors properly hung, we walked up the basement stairs to a waiting car, but Mac wasn't finished. As we made ourselves comfortable in the old Ford, he said, "The next one is Goering to be Hit-larious," but stopped because a platoon of German soldiers had rounded the corner two blocks ahead, heading our way. They saw our car and surrounded us, rifles at the ready.

The sergeant spoke to our driver through the open car window. In German he said, "*Papiere jetzt.*"

I was in the back of the car trying to hide my Royal Air Force uniform, but since I spoke German I translated. Our driver gave his identification paper and his ration card to the German NCO.

The German soldier handed the identification papers back to the driver and said to me, "*Was machst du hier —* what are you doing here?"

I translated and Mac's wife replied in French. My French, improving every day, was good enough to understand. I laughed and looked at the soldier and said, "*Sergeant, mein Deutsch ist gut, aber mein Französisch ist nicht, aber ich werde mein Bestes tun, um ihnen zu sagen, was sie gesagt hat-Sargeant, my German is not very good but my french is. I will do my best to tell you what she said.*" The soldier nodded to Lorraine.

Pointing at Mac's wife, I explained, "*Die schone Dame wurde verschmäht und wir sind hier um Rache zu suchen-The beautiful lady was spurned and we are here to seek revenge.*" The sergeant grimaced and wished us luck. Lorraine had made the right call — Germans understood honour and revenge. Mac, Lorraine and the rest put their pistols away and we continued our journey.

That was my final adventure with Mac and his crew. Being surrounded by German soldiers and escaping only because of quick thinking was too much for me. I knew that if I was captured alone as a uniformed combatant I would be delivered to a camp for prisoners of war. Not fun and exciting, but part of the Geneva Convention. Caught participating in resistance activities and the execution of informants, I would be tortured and then executed as a spy. I decided that I would leave the group, head west towards the English Channel and hope for the best. Clearly the partisans and my friend Mac had work to do and did not need me in the way.

I said goodbye to my friends and left the next morning, borrowing a compass from Mac. His wife Lorraine told me that I was a *putain d'idiot*, kissed both my cheeks and told me that we would meet again.

A week later I was captured.

My Cell, My Prison

Nine out of ten French citizens living in occupied France were patriots willing to help a Royal Air Force pilot who was trying to get to the west coast. They knew that by giving me shelter, food and often transportation, they were jeopardizing the lives of themselves and their families. My weak French was a problem and my ability to speak German a bigger problem, but after a week I found myself in the ruined city of Calais. I hoped to contact the underground there and find a way to return to England and my fighter squadron and the war. Mostly I wanted a Burton ale and some fish and chips soaked in vinegar and wrapped in newspaper.

One out of ten French citizens living in occupied France was not a patriot and was unwilling to help a pilot who had recently been shot down and who wanted his fish and chips and vinegar. Worse, to save themselves and their families, some of the one in ten were willing to sell their soul to the Germans, and the Germans were more than willing to give them thirty pieces of silver in exchange.

An older couple had very willingly given me food and a bed for the night. In the morning the front door was bashed inward, followed by a dozen or so of Germany's finest Waffen Schutzstaffel — the SS. They were very professional and treated me with a certain deference, almost as a brother in arms. The couple demanded payment for turning me in and became loud and abrasive when it was apparent that the promised money was not forthcoming. Both were shot through the head and left in the front garden next to a midden pile.

I sat between two burly soldiers in the back of a staff car. My hands were free and I was drinking schnapps with the commanding officer, who was sitting in the front seat beside the driver. The car windows were down because it was a beautiful, warm day. In a small village we were held up for an hour or so as German troops stomped through the homes and other buildings, searching for something or someone. Eventually loud voices announced that they had been successful in their quest.

A young man holding a young child in his arms was escorted from a small house and forced to stand before a stone wall. The child was crying, and the man looked shaken and very sad. His long black hair flapping in the wind, the man wrapped his entire body about the child in a loving embrace, sheltering it from the soldiers. The man gently said, "*Calme mon agneau*," to the child as they were shot. My escort watched this microcosm of inhumanity unfold from the comfort of the staff car, and I saw sadness and melancholy envelop everyone. They put away the alcohol and were silent for the rest of the trip.

After three days we were met at a checkpoint by a regular army officer and his men, and everything changed for me. An official-looking piece of paper exchanged hands, followed by a hand-off between the SS men who had captured me and the regular German troops. I was confused by this, because I had been told that I was being escorted to a prisoner-of-war camp for British officers, and I was okay with that. But the men who accepted my transfer were rougher and far brusquer than the SS troops who had fed me alcohol and good German sausages.

The new soldiers tied my hands behind my back like a common criminal, and after they threw me into the back of their truck I was beaten with a rubber hose and then driven to a train station. We boarded a train, and after three days of little water and no food we arrived in East Berlin. A car was waiting. I was given another beating and then a short drive to the place where monsters lived and where monsters were made.

The car stopped and I heard a few words in harsh German that I could not make out. The engine was turned off and the trunk was opened, spilling oppression and the smell of blood into the trunk where, I lay handcuffed and sullen. A very fat army private yanked on the restraints, pulling me out of the car and into a large, bricked courtyard. Surrounding the courtyard were high walls manned by soldiers with very big guns, and all those guns were pointed at me. The cuffs were removed, the car started again, and my escort departed the prison.

I was left standing in front of a wooden gallows made for three. A few other prisoners shuffled by, seemingly intent on whatever task or errand that was at the time the pinnacle of their existence. I examined the wooden beams and the planks underneath the noose as I waited and was shocked when I understood that the machine was designed not for a long drop but for an extended, torturous death.

"I am the duty sergeant — *Ich bin direkte hinter* — and you are an *Untermensch*," a man shouted from directly behind me. "Never mind my name, because you will not be here long enough to need it. Understand this and understand it well: you are here in this prison to do one and only one thing, and that is to die. This is an execution facility, not a readjustment centre. *Für dich, endet es hier* — for you, it ends here! The only uncertainty is how we will do it and when we will do it."

With that I received my striped prison outfit and my tattoo, consisting of six numbers: 09 01 40. My Royal Air Force uniform was carefully folded by a soldier wearing a combat helmet who stored it in the main administrative area.

"It ends here" is what the petulant guard told me upon my arrival, and I believed it. It was called Strafgefängnis Plötzensee prison, and I will find it very difficult to say those two horrible words again. The words are abhorrent to me. If I say them again I will vomit. I have no clue how many people lived at that place awaiting their fate, but I soon learned that the guard had been partially correct. Good, brave people came to that place to die, while others who had really pissed off the Nazis came to die horribly.

For the first few weeks most of my time was spent in my cell, which boasted a mouldy mattress and a tiny multi-purpose stool. I was allowed out of my room each day at six p.m. to assist in cleaning up after the hangings that had taken place in the courtyard. Most executions, I soon learned, started at five p.m. and were generally over by 5:45. Some deaths happened in a place referred to by the staff as the "death house"; those endings were not for public consumption. Other deaths occurred incidentally, such as when an inmate irritated a guard, forgot a rule or came to the attention of someone in a bad mood. Of course, starvation and suicide took their fair share of people as well.

Friendships and comradery were out of the question in that prison. What was the point? The goal for each of us, in our own persnickety way, was to manoeuvre through each day without attracting the attention of the worst sadists and hoping that our name would not be read out in the morning to announce our execution in the afternoon.

All of us developed rituals or had homemade talismans to keep the bogeyman at bay. Those mantras and charms always worked until they didn't. Imagine the collective sigh of relief every morning when the more fortunate knew that they had at least thirty-six more hours to live. People today complain about feeling stressed and call anxiety the new psychological disorder or mental illness. But we the walking dead, bustling through our survival protocol or counting our beads, were truly anxious.

Purgatory

Stasis is the word that best illustrates my initial hours, days, and weeks at the prison. That place, which I hope to never again refer to by name, was a prison, not a camp or a concentration camp, although for some that will be an irrelevant distinction. The function of that prison in East Berlin was to dispose of those who angered or terrified the Third Reich. Perhaps *angered* is the wrong word, so I will stick with *terrified*. Ideas and independent thinking worried the Nazi machine, and those not willing to raise their right hand in salute when ordered to scared the Nazis. So the Nazis did what they did best, and that was a systematic, organized, and factory-like elimination of the problem. I am reminded of the trucks I sometimes see as I panhandle and look for food, rumbling along King Street or Highway 8 and carrying pigs to the slaughter factory over in Breslau. At the red light, where the trucks stop for a moment, I look into the eyes of the animals and think about the efficiency that got them into those trucks and then on to a place where they will be disposed of and then forgotten — a problem solved.

It is true that I made no friends or acquaintances

among the other prisoners and guards, but I watched and listened very carefully. The pig who can avoid the hammer to the head is a wise and lucky pig indeed. I learned that the guards believed the Kommandant, the colonel in charge of the prison, had gone insane upon the recent news of the death of his son at the hands of a British fighter pilot. He was said to *nicht mehr alle Tassen im Schrank haben,* which I translated to mean that the camp commander no longer has all his cups in the cupboard. The prison, they whispered, was functioning without his input, and some believed that because of that, mistakes were being made.

The guards, I decided, were the cream of the crap, mostly rejects from fighting units. Those rejects were sadists, alcoholics, rapists, and the lazy, and they hated us, the prisoners. They viewed us as problems to be trussed up and then killed. The inmates, on the other hand, were the cream of German society. They were the brave intellectuals, people who disagreed with the war and had said no to the Nazi political machine. There were also Germans who Hitler had decided were inferior, such as homosexual men and women, but especially outspoken women. Of course, there was always a sprinkling of brave and proud partisans and resistance fighters. These last always suffered the most when their time came to be marched to the death house.

I had no idea under which of the categories I had been placed. I was a Royal Air Force fighter pilot who had been shot down over occupied France, and for a long while I had no idea why I was at that place. I slept, I ate, I listened, and I did exactly as I was told. And of course, I waited.

One sunny afternoon a prisoner arrived by the usual method. He was chained from his shoulders to his ankles and his face and body displayed the signs of a very brutal beating by the Gestapo. None of the prisoners knew who he was, but it was obvious the man had done something extraordinary, judging by the size of the honour guard that escorted him to his cell. We thought nothing more about him because we had our own worries and problems. We were, however, surprised next morning when nobody was listed to be executed that afternoon. A prisoner standing deathly still beside me whispered from the side of his mouth, "*Etwas Besonderes, ich denke Tods.*" I agreed that something special had been planned.

At four-thirty the guards began to yell for all the prisoners to gather in front of the wooden gibbet. The centre hook had a rope threaded through it and a noose was suspended over a large chair. At five p.m. the man who had arrived the day before was dragged to the gibbet and held in place on the chair (a stool, really). A small piece of paper spattered in blood had been pinned to his chest, but I could not read what it said. A noose was quickly placed around the man's neck and without ceremony the stool was very tenderly removed from underneath his feet. He dangled and choked for a few minutes as we watched. A prisoner in the front row looked away for a moment and was struck viciously on the head with a club, killing him.

The stool was replaced under the condemned man's feet and he was held very carefully by four guards. The noose was loosened, and the man slowly regained his ability to breathe properly. At a signal from the window of the Kommandant's office, the man was rehanged, and then rehanged again, and then again. Eventually the wretch was dead. As he was being removed from the scaffolding, the prisoners, the witnesses to this shameless torture, shuffled to their cells in silence. A small work party of inmates, including me, stayed behind to clean up. That man must have really scared somebody to be murdered four times.

Condemned

At six p.m. forty-two days after that brutal execution, I was at my post removing blood and other things from underneath the gallows when three guards pulled me to my feet and dragged me to the office of the Commander, the chief warden of the prison. I had seen the *Oberstleutnant* — the colonel — a few times staring at me from his office window as he smoked his cigarette, with a look of hatred marring what perhaps had once been a happy face. The obligatory Charlie Chaplin moustache was positioned just so under long protruding nostril hairs. I was worried why I had attracted his attention. My heart was pounding; I vomited onto the front of my prison uniform and received a punch from one of the guards for doing so.

Hands pinned behind my back, I was placed directly in front of an oak desk, the camp commander sitting on the opposite side. The Colonel worked on his Nazi papers for a long time before speaking to me. His jaw was clenched, and I saw cruelty and violence held in check by pure Nazi willpower. He slowly lifted his eyes in my direction; I looked down as his gaze lifted upwards. Our eyes met in a brief transaction, but I knew not yet the coinage.

"I have always hated the Royal Air Force," the Chief Warden said mildly. With that statement he had acknowledged that I was not a spy but a combatant, and I relaxed a little. Perhaps, I reasoned, I had been called to this office to be informed that I was being sent to an air force prisoner-of-war camp. Which one would it be, I wondered, and then remembered that my hands were tied. Good news seldom comes in tandem with restraints.

"Look at me, Flying Officer Gerald Kurt Paine. Yes, I know who you are, and I know what you have done." He glanced very briefly at a family portrait hanging on the wall to his left: the colonel, a smiling woman, and a handsome young man wearing a Luftwaffe uniform.

I looked over the man's shoulder through the filthy window to the courtyard and waited. I remember being very warm in that office and becoming very worried.

"Yes, I know you quite well, Gerald Kurt Paine. When you were picked up, I asked a favour of the Schutzstaffel and had you brought to this place — my place. Do you have any idea how much those parasites will want in return? You may answer."

I didn't know what to say. He knew who I was, and he had convinced the scariest and most radical military organization in Germany to deliver me to that exact spot, in front of that exact desk. I answered his question, anxious as hell not to make things worse. "I can only imagine. What have I done? Why am I here, sir?"

The man sneered. "You think I should send you, a combatant, to a soldier's prison?"

"Yes, sir, I do."

He stood abruptly, strode around his desk, and struck me on the side of my head with his baton. When I backed away, he kicked me in the stomach. The colonel began to scream like a banshee, "You are not a soldier! You are a criminal, a vile, vicious criminal, a base, corrupt, evil devil — a murderer!"

I was on the floor, vomiting again and bleeding from an open wound on my head. I noticed other stains from other people soaked into the wood, dark and ominous. My offerings blended perfectly into that Rorschach artwork of despair and pain. As I was hauled to my feet by the friendly guards, who until now had been hovering at attention behind me, I saw a ghoul's head laughing at me. My head and stomach hurt, and I was heartsick with anxiety. For five minutes I continued to retch, then ten.

Suddenly the Commandant spoke again. His anger had not been moderated by my artwork on the floor. He sat perched on his desk, his eyes inches from mine. "Yes, you are *ficken böse*. Tomorrow you will be hung from a rope until your miserable, evil life ends. Then I will feed you to the camp dogs. After they shit you out, I will mix the filth with the piss and shit in the latrine. I will think of you every time I take a *Scheisse*." He nodded and I was taken away.

A Table, a Chair, a Fork and Breakfast

Early the next morning I was escorted to the death house holding area. It was a very dim, forlorn space, about twelve feet by sixteen feet, with the only light meandering its way from two very small windows near the ceiling. It wasn't until my eyes had adjusted to the lack of light that I saw among the prisoners my friend MacDonald, sitting with his head in his hands. I knew it was him by the missing finger.

A cold metal bench was attached to a cement wall opposite the door; another, shorter bench decorated the wall to the left. Each of us was cuffed to a rusted metal ring screwed deeply into the walls. I mused to myself that it would be impossible to nap and that it was just another form of torture. MacDonald sat upright when I gently called his name. He looked over my shoulder and past me with a four-thousand-mile westward gaze. I remember feeling very sad for my friend.

We had been told not to speak, so I whispered, "Your wife?"

Mac nodded. "She is fine. Lorraine was in town

getting food when the soldiers surrounded the house. I lived; others did not. Pierre is here too, and some others from our group. We were sold out to the Gestapo by some fine French citizens. You know the saying — *J'irai le a la Commandant.*"

"How long have you been here, at this place?" I asked.

"Two days. The People's Court sentenced us to die for crimes against the people of the Third Reich, et cetera, et cetera."

"I am so sorry, my friend. We will die together as comrades and brothers — you, me, Pierre, and the others," I whispered and tried to reach him, but could not. Mac smiled and put his head back into his hands.

At noon a camp flunky, a *Lager Laufer*, announced, "The prisoners will listen, as Herr Feldwebel will now speak." A prison sergeant strode into the room with the usual Nazi bravado and ceremony. He clicked the heels of his boots together. We all stared at the boots. To us, who always hung our heads when addressed by any of the German prison staff, boots, those ugly, highly polished black boots, when pointing at you and not moving quickly away, meant death. We knew by the boots what Herr Sergeant was about to tell us before he even opened his mouth to speak through his rotting teeth. I did not see his mouth move because I could not shift my eyes or my thoughts from the boots inches from my own feet. Perhaps, like the others, I was hoping that by inspecting the jackboots so solicitously I would become invisible.

The owner of those boots spoke very loudly. "Prisoners will listen very carefully. Failure to listen will result in a beating." He pointed to one of the other guards, who held a wooden club with jagged edges and dark stains. I did not need to see the weapon because, one beautiful morning two days ago, that ash club had caved in a man's skull because he was whistling a jaunty French melody.

The Nazi NCO laughed and continued. "You are condemned spies, and this afternoon at five o'clock you will be executed by hanging." He pointed down the hall to a black door that led outside and continued, "At five minutes to five p.m. you will strip and fold your clothes neatly. A hood will be placed over your head. You will form a line and be taken out that door and then across the courtyard to the death house. There you will be hanged." The bastard paused for a full minute and then continued his pronouncement. "You will slowly strangle to death."

We continued to stare at his boots. I noticed a small brown stain on the toe of his left boot and was glad. None of us reacted to his announcement, because we did not want to invite any special attention from this sadist.

The black boots were still talking at us. "Today you will think about the harm you have done to the Third Reich. You may not talk and will be allowed no opportunity to relieve yourself. You can shit yourself now or while choking."

Then the boots stomped away and we breathed again. Nobody talked that day, and nobody shit themselves.

The incipient hope that I had been preserving in my heart since my abrupt arrival at that prison vanished. My stomach heaved with the bile and acid that had accumulated in my guts when the man in the dark boots officially announced our deaths. I felt tiny flies crawling along my colon, searching for my end. I did not want to die. I wanted to see my family and friends and I wanted to fly my little airplane. I wanted to show my friend Mac all the best places to drink beer and meet willing women. I wanted Mac and me to dig Jennifer from her tomb and revive her. I wanted to grow old, learn to smoke strong cigarettes, and retell the story about the time I got drunk with the King of

England. No, I did not want to die in that terrible place.

For the rest of the afternoon, I listened as my friend sang a sad French song over and over. The others looked at the floor, dust motes floating around them in the dim light and stale air.

At one minute to five, naked and hooded, we were marched into the death house. Once inside we were turned slightly, marched forward, and turned again, gently this time, as if by a corrective schoolmaster. A hand grasped the top of my head and I startled. The vomit-smelling hood was removed from my head, taking with it strands of filthy hair, and was replaced by a red hood with small holes for my eyes and a large hole for my mouth. The others continued to wear the death bags.

The place of execution was the size of a large class-room, windowless, with large, glaring lights on the ceiling. I, a doomed man, stared in horror, because two terrible events were happening at the same time. To my left stood a guillotine with a headless naked body on a steel table and a head in a large steel bucket off to one side, awash in blood. Three naked men waited their turn in line, hands and thighs tied securely, standing as still as death and trying not to fall over. Each man was looking anywhere but at the staring head in the bucket or the headless body that was streaming blood onto the autopsy table.

On our side of the room, eight meat hooks were suspended from the ceiling very close to the back wall. Our murderers had expertly positioned each of us a metre from a hook, facing away from it. The others were unaware where they were standing. Besides the sergeant and our colour parade, three men stood grimly facing our way. They wore the usual dark uniform, creased in the usual way, but each wore a rubber apron tied in front. The leader held in his hands a piece of thin rope with a loop at each end.

A small desk and chair had been positioned in front of the first hook on the right. On the desk a plate of sausages and scrambled eggs had been carefully positioned so the eater of that meal would face the cruel hooks. A very large gold fork completed the breakfast ensemble. My friend MacDonald had been placed under that first hook, and when I looked his way, his mask was removed. A guard grabbed my shoulders and shoved me over to the desk, where I was forced to sit in the chair, the meal inches from my chest. Large hands on my shoulders kept me in place. It was then that I noticed the Luftwaffe symbol embossed carefully into the handle of the fork.

The first six heroes of that afternoon were hanged. My friend MacDonald remained under his hook and watched as they kicked, twitched, and gagged. Some tried to live a little longer by positioning their feet on the back wall, but doing so made their torment last much longer. Eventually the twitching and gagging stopped, and the men were still, their heads tilted grotesquely to the right.

At this point the camp commander entered. He sighed and, not looking at me but at the wall behind the dead prisoners, said, "Flying Officer, eat the eggs and sausage and you can leave this room and this prison. A car awaits outside." I reached for the fork with my left hand, but it was stopped by a guard. He had pliers ready and ripped out a fingernail. I cried like a child.

The Commander laughed and thanked his subordinate. He continued, "I had not finished speaking. You Canadians are so impolite. As I was going to say, if you eat the breakfast while you watch your friend hang, you may go. I said *while*, not before and not after. I said *while* he hangs and dies."

With that my best friend was hoisted off his feet and dangled from a hook. We locked eyes, and for a precious moment I shared his suffering. Then he looked elsewhere and was on his own, while I vomited on the table in front of me.

I did not eat the food and was taken back to my cell. My little finger was bloody and painful, and I knew for a certainty they would do that again.

My Lessons Begin

Next morning I was escorted to the prison commander's office for the second time. The Chief Warden stood in front of his desk, but his back was towards the door and the man was looking at something outside the window. A small table had been pushed against the desk and on it a beautiful new violin was waiting. Another small table was nestled against the back wall with a chair in front. On the table the gold fork pointed at the breakfast I had refused to eat the day before. Congealed vomit and bile covered the food.

"Paine, the breakfast will remain until you eat it. Then you can go home. Eat it, my son, and then we can go home. Eat."

I knew that I would be broken if I ate the slop on that table. I thought about my friend for a moment and said, "No, sir, I will not. I cannot."

"Then choose from the other table and pick up the instrument. You will play for me today."

I had no difficulty holding the fine instrument despite my injured finger, but I could not produce music from that or any musical instrument. I could repair farm machinery and fly an airplane, but I could not do as he demanded. "Sorry, but I cannot play," I said to the man who held the power of death or life over me.

"Do not refuse my wishes twice today. You will play for me today," he repeated in the same tone. I hesitated, not knowing what to say or do. He turned from the window, walked to the place where I was standing, and struck me on the face with his open hand. "My son, my boy, you will play when I tell you to play, as I have told you many times before." He took the violin from me, placed it gently under my chin, and positioned my hands just so. Again, I could not play. I was beaten again.

All day long I was smacked and beaten because I could not play, and my blood and sweat dripped constantly onto the floor. I had never had much skill with such things, and the more he struck me, the more mistakes I made. I could barely hold the instrument.

"Perhaps, Herr Kommandant, your son needs a drink to help reorganize his thoughts," the guard standing at the door suggested.

"Yes, yes, give my son some schnapps. Some schnapps should do it. Yes, yes, some schnapps should do it," the warden agreed. "Give my good boy something to revive his ability, and then take him to his room to rest and recover. I don't know what has happened. He should be able to play. He has played since he was a little boy."

Private Alvin, the guard who had saved me, hesitated a minute at my cell door. He clearly wanted to tell me something.

I asked, "Private, what is it you wish to tell me? I will listen. Go ahead."

"Flying Officer Paine, I was there when they told him about his son and how he died. Do you wish to know about this, since it concerns you?" he asked, his hands resting on the windowsill.

"Yes, *Soldat* Alvin, I do."

"I am in the office every day, but he has always viewed

me as a piece of furniture and not a man, or even a human. When the messenger arrived from the Luftwaffe to inform him that his son had been killed by the Royal Air Force, I was there pretending to be a chair and I watched and listened. You understand what I am saying, Flying Officer Paine?"

Again "Yes" was my response.

The soldier, after nodding to himself, said, "His son was a good man and had prepared his father for the possibility, but at that moment, as the messenger stood at attention in front of him, it was more than he could bear. The Kommandant paced about the room and began to scream and scream, 'My son, my boy, my baby son! He is dead, gone, and never to be seen again!'"

It was very easy to imagine the camp *Kommandant* reacting that way, and I said nothing.

Private Alvin sighed and continued, "He grabbed the messenger by the collar of his uniform and spat in his face. He told the man from the Luftwaffe — a boy really, with bad teeth and terrible acne — that he could have him shot for the way he was standing. The boy was terrified and clearly wanted to placate the grieving father in front of him and escape any insane order that he might give at any moment, but he did not know how. I suggested to the Kommandant that he let the messenger return to his duties, and eventually the young man was told to leave. Then I watched as the Kommandant called people he knew in the Luftwaffe and the SS. Pilot Paine of the Royal Air Force, do you understand what was happening?"

"Yes and no," I replied. It was then that I noticed that the guard had placed a pair of large flying goggles over his eyes.

More and More

The camp *Kommandant* continued the insane liturgy the next day and the next, with only minor variations in the expectations and outcome. It was apparent that he thought I was his son and should be able to play the violin. Yet every so often his mind would clear, and he would address me as Gary Paine, former Royal Air Force pilot. He would scream at me that I had done something terrible, either to Germany or to him.

He would flit back and forth between evil pilot and bad son. It was a confusing, anxious time for me, not knowing if I was to be beaten for being his incompetent child or to be hung for being myself, a criminal Royal Air Force pilot. The man was clearly insane and it had become his personal goal to destroy me, his "son." Because of that I refused to consume the rotting sausage and egg with vomit sauce.

After the fourth or fifth day of torment, my skills with the violin remaining nonexistent, I was escorted by the office guard, Alvin, not to the camp commander's office but again to the death house. My breakfast was sitting where it had been for Mac's death, in front of the first hook. Eight condemned prisoners were brought in with death bags over their heads. Again, my torturer offered freedom if I ate the now mouldy breakfast as they were being hanged. Again, I refused and again a fingernail was removed. I knew it was coming this time and controlled my screams by thinking about flying Jenny and dropping orange pumpkin bombs onto the prison.

This became the pattern of my life: Violin "lessons" and beatings and executions that I witnessed while sitting at my breakfast table. In time my fingernails and toenails grew back, only to be torn out again and again. I was a handsome man, but the scars from the beatings in the office as I made squeaks on the strings were slowly turning me into something else.

I know all this sounds far-fetched and ridiculous, but what happened to me at that prison, in that puke-smelling office and that awful room of death, is true, and what I am telling you is true. It happened. It happened, I am certain of it. It got worse — far worse — and in the end I did not survive.

Vomit Sauce

For the next year, every day from 9:00 in the morning until 4:55 in the afternoon, I stood in front of the Warden, refused to eat the breakfast, and learned to play the violin. I was being broken on a wheel of music and pain, but I became almost able to play. Being able to play meant that I could more often avoid the bloody baton.

One day early in the morning, I missed a chord and was hit on my left wrist for my transgression. It was a mild rebuke and expected, and I deserved it. It was my fault, as it had been me that made the error. I tried again and got it correct and was rewarded by not being hit again, which of course, when you are a prisoner, is the best kind of reward.

The colonel turned his attention from me to the stack of papers on the left side of his desk and then to the smaller stack on the right. He sighed and glanced at his watch. Since by then I knew his routines, he and I both understood that his work and my practising had hours to go until we could stop for the day. The commander picked up the next paper and I saw that it was a warrant for the execution of prisoners in Cell D. It required a wax seal with his name in ink underneath. He always used a black pen with blood-red ink for death warrants.

The brassy noise of guards bullying prisoners in a work party disturbed the *Oberstleutnant's* thoughts and he looked outside with irritation. A frail prisoner was being kicked in the stomach after he had tripped on the icy ground and fallen onto his back. I had witnessed the man falling, the quick, arrogant anger of the guards, and the assault.

The prisoner did not scream or cry, knowing that to do so would result in immediate death. Like all of us when at the mercy of sadistic anger, the prisoner merely hoped that the abuse would end before bones were broken or vital organs pierced. He and I had been through the ritual before and knew that sadism must be satisfied before the day could continue. I was not surprised when the man quickly turned onto his stomach so he could vomit without choking. One quiet cough (we had learned to do that) and the contents of his stomach decorated the harsh, filthy ground. The man's breakfast gruel was thoroughly mixed with whatever had fallen from the bottom of the guard's filthy jackboots.

Tired of his pastime, the guard stopped kicking and swaggered away smiling, having immediately forgotten about the wretch he had almost murdered. He would not have used that word; he would have said *exterminated.* The prisoner waited until the guard was gone and then scooped the vomit and dirt into his cupped hands and ate the prison porridge as fast as he was able.

The *Oberstleutnant* did not appear bothered by the beating or the prisoner's quick retrieval of what was rightly his. Prisoners were nothing to the *Oberstleutnant*, just spies, Russians, sexual deviants, and anyone who had said no to the Nazi machine. All were awaiting their moment on the hook or the meat slicer.

We had both stopped what we were doing to watch the

grotesque burlesque. He spoke to me while staring again at his papers. On this day, as on many and ever-increasing numbers of days, he thought I was his dead son, or possibly his ghost. "Sometimes, my son, I am fascinated by the absurd symbolism of eating vomit." He smiled and added, "Look at this pile of paper from Berlin that also must be eaten and then regurgitated all over the prison and sent to headquarters with our shit and dirt mixed into it."

Another Day, Another Lesson

The warden seemed to be in a good mood the following day, and the slash with his baton had not resulted in much of a mark. He searched my face, trying to recognize me, and told me to play a few easy chords. When I had finished, he said, "I suppose it is time, Herr Murderer Hurricane pilot, to tell you about my boy, who, like you, signed up to fight from the left seat of an airplane, a Henkel bomber. You know this aircraft, I think."

I nodded very slightly because he was correct, I knew that killing machine very well.

The Kommandant did not like my nod and gripped the lapels of my prisoner's jacket and yanked me onto the tips of my toes. "Well, murderer, do you know this aircraft?" Spit exploded from the back of his throat. I could see that little worm thing wiggle as he spoke. "Answer me, Canadian bastard! Answer me!"

"Yes, I know the airplane. I shot one down once," I answered him.

He asked, "Did the crew escape after you destroyed the Henkel?"

"No."

"How do you know that none survived, that none

bailed out?" he asked.

I was puzzled by the question and answered truthfully. "Because I followed the bomber to the ground and emptied my magazine into it until it crashed."

The prison warden stared at me and nodded his head as if confirming something. "Eat the breakfast, Paine, and my son and you can both live," he implored.

"No."

The man took the violin from me and placed it next to the breakfast. He turned to the window and then turned back again to where I stood, hoping to be returned to my cell. His face and body had changed. He was not the Kommandant but something evil and malevolent, if that was possible. He screamed at me in German and English and then began his attack. Sometimes the kicks and cuts were because I was a Canadian bastard; other times, in guttural German, I was his son, sometimes twelve years old and sometimes older.

My mind became detached from the pain after thirty minutes or so by the old clock in the corner. I noticed that the attack was far more vicious and uncompromising when he saw me as his young son. This beating would have ended me if the Kommandant had not become exhausted by his efforts.

No medical treatment was offered as I was carried to my cell, except by the ever-present office guard, Alvin. He cleaned the blood from my face and I did not feel the crude stitching as he tried to stop the bleeding from my left cheek and torso. He told me that two ribs had been broken, that the baton cuts would heal, and that I would live — this time.

The man seemed to wear his stupid helmet day and night, and in time I would understand why. And around his neck always hung the flying goggles.

Torture

Executions did not happen every day. The Nazis performed a kind of pantomime where they would await an execution order from someplace in Berlin. Thousands were murdered, some outside in the cold and some in the death room. I was there for all the hangings in that room. The Warden was trying to break me as punishment for killing his son. This I knew for a certainty now, but he was also trying to break me as his real son, for things the boy had done to embarrass his father. The Warden was insane, and he was a monster, but for a long time I would not allow him to break me, would not allow him to break us.

All the executions in the death house happened as I watched from my desk. My constant companions were the mouldy meat and the dried-out eggs. "As you watch, eat, and you can go home, Pilot Paine of the Royal Air Force. Eat and I will forgive you, my son," the man/monster would say gently, like a patient parent dealing with a stupid child. His insanity was palpable.

My answer was always "No, I will not." I watched each hero die, then held out a hand for the bastard with the pliers to rip off a fingernail. Later it became toenails and eventually the ends of my toes; later still it was strips of skin from anywhere on my body except my face and hands. My fingers were needed to play the violin. I have no idea why he did not take skin from my face.

The breakfast meal would be moved to the Warden's office when I played the instrument, and then to my cell, and then to wherever I might be, including the latrine area. The monster wanted me always to see the breakfast and eat the meal and become something that scurries in the night. The man also wanted to kill his son.

Coffee Smells

I have held on to certain odours all these years, in the hope that by doing so I will retain a modicum of sanity in an insane world. What smells am I referring to? Why, they are the flatus of dread and hopelessness begotten by impending pain, torture, and death. I knew them as lovers and givers in a different place and time.

The smells. I sometimes sit alone, my steel cover tilted slightly back on my head and loose at the chin, on a plastic chair in that famous, red-striped doughnut coffee shop created by a famous leaf, close my eyes, and gently sniff. Generally, people look away when I do that and have nervous breakdowns. I smell the room again, and quickly the fragrances of despair drench me in the juice of memory and I feed very gently. At the same time I watch doughnut lovers obediently form that famous doughnut queue from the door to the place where it all happens. Ah. I blink and see condemned prisoners on their way to the hemp and the hooks. I see my friend MacDonald and the German traitors, the innocent and the brave.

I understand the stink. It is adrenaline, urine, shit, apocrine glands creating death proteins, and of course the oldies but goodies: bacteria from the groin, armpits, and around the nipples creating proteins and bacteria. I am glad that I still recall the smells. It means that I am not yet immune to compassion and am still a tiny bit human. Ha! Or perhaps it means that I am not human at all.

It was a cold November day as a death-room sergeant positioned me at the table with the fork dominating its smooth surface. The side door — the door that opened only when blood and despair were imminent — was swung inward by a smiling corporal with gold fillings dominating his front teeth. It was then that the stink entered the death room and stayed for a while. I glanced down the hallway and saw that the doughnut line was perfectly straight and that each of the five doomed heroes wore a cloth bag over his head and had his legs tied at the thighs and hands tied in front. They were naked because a man without his clothes, a man humiliated by removal of his last vestige of civilization, is easier to kill. It's hard to be arrogant and proud with your cock and balls dangling and swaying. It was the Nazi way.

A while ago I had been in that line. What had I been thinking as I stood waiting for my chocolate doughnut with darkness around me and my own stink to keep me company? The truth — and I love truth when I can find it lurking somewhere deep in my deluded mind — is that I had stopped thinking the moment those arrogant pricks placed me in the doughnut line.

Back to doughnuts and meat hooks for a moment. My question: What do you think about as you wait in line for a doughnut? The answer: nothing. Nothing at all, because you are merely waiting. Waiting in a doughnut line for hell or waiting for pleasure, it is the same, because you are waiting for something inevitable. Next time you find your-self in a line, try to think. You will not be able to do it. This all sounds preposterous, but I know what I am talking about.

You are wondering, how can waiting patiently and respectfully in line to have a rope placed around your neck and to be hoisted a foot off the ground be the same as waiting for a doughnut? Well, I've done both, so I know they are the same. It's just a matter of behaving your-self in line as you wait to get your reward. Now you are saying, *This guy is nuts*. But I say to you, I was in that line in the dank, smelly hallway waiting to die and I have waited for a doughnut, so shut up and bloody think about what I have been saying!

I am perhaps the only person who understands the truth of what I allude to. In each case, it is working for a reward. Your safe, middle-class mind that has never been to war and never witnessed or been part of the horror is strongly disputing what I allude to because, after all, in your world rewards are always good things, something earned. And you are so right, but think. I say again, think — think using Occam's razor. (Sorry, you will have to use the stupid Internet to understand the razor.)

I suspect that you continue to not understand. Nobody ever does, so here is the answer to the death-line-and-doughnut riddle. It is simple, and it is a truth: If you behave in the doughnut line by being obedient and quiet and mannerly, you just might receive more than the doughnut you ordered, including some kindness or a smile from the overworked and underappreciated person dealing with you. If you are quiet and obedient and mannerly while in line awaiting pain and suffering, you may be rewarded with a bit of decency or kindness. If you are extra good, the guards might even pull on your legs once you are suspended by your neck with the rope cutting into your throat, thus ending your misery a little sooner. Do you understand, then, that kindness can be different in different situations, and why I sometimes see my friend Mac at the doughnut shop being good as he shuffles forward to take his turn? But perhaps I am wrong and the doughnut-line people are more obedient yet receive less reward.

From my cell window I watched the guards wait in line for a bit of alcohol after the exertions of picking up victims and attaching them to hooks. They were exhausted from their remedial weightlifting. But a line is a line, waiting is waiting, and hopes are hopes. It was amazing to watch monsters, who moments before had lurched and killed, form their own beautiful line and stand obedient and respectful, hoping for a little kindness or a reward of extra schnapps.

Piano Wire is too Merciful

"I am an unrepentant Nazi and will be until the end. And believe me, the end is near. We have a year or two at most, and then those invited to the gallows party will be wearing a different kind of uniform. After all, it is now May 1944 and an invasion is imminent. That will be the beginning of the end, I am certain. Until then, for me at least, it will be business as usual and good deeds done. Ha!"

I had entered the *Oberstleutnant*'s office moments before. I seemed to be listening to the middle of a diatribe that had begun long before my appearance. I watched as the camp commander shrugged and smiled. He took a deep breath and changed the topic of his philosophical onslaught. "Well, prisoner with identification number 09 01 40, perhaps it is time to tell you about the one thing in life that gives me purpose and a reason to breathe and do this useful work."

He gestured to his desk and said, "And what work is that? you might ask, prisoner 09 01 40. Why, it is to disgorge these stupid papers and rid the world of *those*." He pointed at his desk and then through the dirty glass of his window to the newly arrived prisoners awaiting induction and disposal. "I eat these pages and dispose of the vomit in memory of my son, the memories of a beautiful boy and a great man."

The warden turned to his assistant, who was always

hovering near the door, always waiting for an order or a sign from his superior. "Private Alvin, give me another word for 'memory' but with more tenebrosity, if you please." Alvin had been a lawyer before the war but was now an ordinary soldier and so was a perfect assistant.

Alvin knew that as a subordinate in the Wehrmacht he was obliged to execute orders immediately and with his best effort. He also understood his boss and knew what he needed. After a moment's hesitation he said, "*Jawohl, Herr Oberstleutnant.* How about 'dark reflections'?" Alvin saluted his superior and clicked his heels. It seemed to me that he had been insolent with that response, or perhaps ironic.

The commander turned to his assistant and glowered, perhaps having the same thoughts that I was having. Abruptly he turned back to me and sighed and said, "'Dark reflections' is accurate. Is the mordancy too much for you, prisoner?" He laughed at this jibe.

I stayed rigid to hide my growing anxiety. It was a bad sign when the colonel became philosophical and emotional.

The colonel looked at his family photograph, static and lost in time, and mused to himself. "Memories can be clear or dark and can be deep or shallow, or more, or less." He sat down and opened a fresh bottle of schnapps. His bleary eyes wandered the room, eventually locating me again in front of his desk. He told me to leave.

At the door he stopped me and said, *"Für dich, endet es hier."* He repeated, "It all ends here." I heard sobbing as I was hustled out of the room.

Fuck and goddamn, I swore silently as I was escorted to my cell. My anxiety had turned to dread and foreboding. Alvin said nothing as he locked the door.

My sleep that night was interrupted by a cell guard

who pulled me to my feet and screamed, "*Stillstehen!*" I quickly stood to attention at the foot of my cot.

Ten minutes later my violin instructor walked into the tiny room. He was clearly drunk and very maudlin. The bastard sneered and then informed me that I was to be executed the next day at five p.m. He then clicked his heels for some reason and left, leaving me with the guard, who shrugged and locked my door.

That was my second execution proclamation, and I was worried because the message had been delivered by the colonel himself. I lay on the floor of my cell until morning.

The group awaiting execution the next day were not the usual assortment of people who frightened the Nazis. They were obviously, judging by their demeanour and arrogance, German military officers. They sat apart from each other and stared at nothing all day, deep within their own dark reflections or possibly playing the old *woulda coulda shoulda* game. At least once during that warm day, every man placed his hands about his neck, anticipating the rope. I did the same more than once, because I believed that was my last day.

Executions were never late and never early, as I have explained before. At precisely 4:55 p.m. the door to our holding area swung open and the killing ritual began. I was accustomed to a certain routine with the actions of the guards, but that day I was shocked when, after we stripped, instead of a crimson hood with eyeholes and mouth hole, they placed a regular black death mask over my head. My hands began to shake, and as we marched across the court-yard to the killing chamber I could not keep my head erect, but let it hang forward like an uncooked German pork sausage. I was sure I was going to die this time, choke to death as the nexus of the cord tightened and tightened. I cried and whimpered and did my own *woulda shoulda.*

I entered that damp place with the smell that during my stay at the prison I could never quite recognize. Years later I realized I had been smelling a strong disinfectant called Dettol, or chloroxylenol (nowadays I call the odour "satanic farts"). However, I did not smell sausage or eggs as I passed through the door into the chamber, and I was not escorted to my usual place at the table but was shoved to a spot underneath a metal hook.

I waited, and as I waited my breathing became frantic and shallow. A thin rope was placed around my neck and I knew that the other end also had a small noose. I listened as this was being done to the others as well, with Nazi precision. I tried to be brave, but lost the struggle. I cried and wished it was the next day, that the coming agony would be over and I would not be a human anymore, just a lump of meat, blood, and shit with no thoughts, no worries, no more struggles to stay sane, no more violin lessons.

I heard the heavy breathing of the assistants as they lifted the first man off the floor so the executioner could attach the rope to a meat hook. I heard a quick intake of breath as the man's breathing was sharply curtailed by the tightening strand of rope. Then I heard the next man being lifted and the next, until I felt the thick fingers of the helpers dig into the pits of my arms like two diddlers having their way with me. Then I felt my legs dangling and the cord biting like a dog at my throat, and I could not breathe. After a few minutes or decades I felt shadows sneaking through the cruel rope and into my brain, about to steal my life.

"Take down prisoner 09 01 40," the camp commander barked. "Do it immediately!" I did not care at that point about anything, because I was happily flying my Curtiss Jenny upside down while drinking a sweet German lager with a straw and trying not to laugh.

x x x

I awoke and saw the leering face of the camp doctor. He said, "You are a fortunate young man, prisoner 09 01 40. Another minute and they would be taking you out there." He pointed to the gate that led to a man in a white lab coat standing by a large open truck. "A strange day — the *Oberstleutnant* condemns you and then saves you. Yes, a strange happenstance. I see that you have fully recovered, so I will be off to supper. Goodbye."

A truth: suffering only counts if you remember the suffering afterwards. If you suffer and then die, what's the point? The doctor had gone for supper with his nice Nazi family and I lay on the floor of my cell understanding the truth of this for the first time. That terrible man who had told me he was a hard-bitten, hard-boiled, impenitent member of the race of right-wing masturbators had taught me the lesson. It is an admonition that I have not forgotten. I am ninety-eight years old and living in a box under a bridge, dictating this story to my friend, and I live that ideal. What's the point of suffering if it is terminal? To torture someone to death is for the torturer; to torture someone and let them live is for the victim. Or is it the other way around?

Must I Then

I realized the next day, while on my way to my violin lesson, that I was not going to physically die in that prison, and that my suffering, moral and otherwise, was just beginning — and I knew why.

My tutor was in a jovial, almost manic mood when I entered the room. "Welcome and good morning, young pilot. I'm glad to see that you are alive and well. Have you eaten? Perhaps not, with your recent accident."

When I shook my head, he pointed to the plate of sausages and eggs perched atop my death-room table. Quietly he said, "Ah, we forgot about your meal yesterday afternoon. Perhaps you would like to eat it now as you remember your most recent *savoir faire*. No? Not yet? Another time, I am certain."

He and I knew that when I ate the breakfast, it would mean that I had been broken on his wheel of hate. Worse — much worse — I would become one of them, one of the monsters. Broken is broken, but a monster is a creature of the dark who eats the *essentia* of others.

The *Oberstleutnant* indicated a different table and, in many ways, a different choice. On it was a violin, and not the beautiful instrument with which I was becoming quite proficient. This offering was an old, scarred, unpolished implement, taken from a deceased inmate, I assumed. It was garbage, and that was how the *Oberstleutnant* saw me: as trash.

"Please pick it up," the *Oberstleutnant* ordered. I should not have touched it, but I carefully took it from the table and held it with disdain in front of me.

"I see that you do not like this violin. It was my son's violin and I would like you to practise with it. The other has been dismantled, along with those traitors who were hanged beside you yesterday. Play 'Must I Then,' the folk-song that you have learned. 'Must I Then' was the first song my son learned to play. Play it, prisoner number 09 01 40. Play it for me, my son."

As I played, he sang along in German. The English translation is something like this:

Must I then, must I then,
Leave this little town, little town,
And you, my dear, stay here?
If I come, if I come,
If I come back again, come back again,
To you I'll rush, my dear.
If I cannot always be right near,
Still your love's my joy, I swear;
If I come, if I come,
If I come back again, come back again,
To you I'll rush, my dear.

I played the song very slowly, as a lament, in C major, with no sharps or flats. The *Oberstleutnant* had a beautiful baritone voice that fit neatly into the pocket created by the music. As he sang I could see that he became the father — my father, the father of the Luftwaffe pilot that I had killed. The room was very quiet when we finished. I placed the violin back on the table and waited.

The *Oberstleutnant* nodded his head and said, "Thank you, my dearest son. That reminded me of the day you left to pilot your bomber to England. That was a nice warm, sunny September day. September 1, 1940." The Colonel shook his head, stared for a moment at my tattoo and then westward out his dirty window, and said, "Off you go, then, and remember to be safe over England and come back to me."

The Commander had continued to juxtapose his son and me. His vengeance against me was confused with his need to punish his son for some reason, and I was certain I knew the reason. He viewed both of us as corrupt and obscene and he needed something that neither of us could deliver.

I returned to my cell not thinking about his delusions

but about the violin. It had created the most beautiful sounds I had ever heard. The notes were ambrosial. I wondered whether in time it would seduce my soul or be my salvation.

Courage

There was another incident viewed from the office window that you should understand. By then I had seen a lot happen from the sanctity of the office, the violin my musical talisman. A woman, starving and stressed, slapped a guard across the face after he ripped open her prison garb, exposing her breasts. Touching a guard was punishable by immediate death, and everyone watching froze into place, awaiting the inevitable. The woman, still angry, struck the leering guard again, but this time it was a kick to the testicles. It was the second most defiant act I witnessed that afternoon, and in many ways it shamed all of us.

The punishment was referred to by the prisoners as the "twenty-five whacks." The guards used clubs and iron bars to break the woman's legs and back and then loaded her onto a cart, which they wheeled towards the outdoor gibbet. The most defiant act that day was when the woman used a razor blade she had hidden in her hair to slice her wrists and throat. She died before the bastards could kill her.

Rice

We now call it obsessive compulsive disorder. My teacher, my father, my jailor, my torturer had many forms of OCD, perhaps his final and (obviously) futile attempts to hang on to a grain of sanity as the hourglass emptied its contents forever. I have waited until now to tell you about this because, compared to other things — other, terrible things — it is trivial. Yes, trivial, but perhaps it demonstrates the disintegration of his mind and how something as small as a grain of rice can determine an outcome.

Each morning, in a pre–music lesson ritual only he could fathom, he created a carefully shaped pile of rice in the middle of his desk. With a magnifying glass in his left hand, he then placed each grain carefully into a large red ceramic bowl with his right hand. Each placement was unique, but in all the months I spent watching this sacrament, I could not detect a pattern or sequence.

A daily tally was kept on a page of the black ledger that he used to record deaths due to execution. The counting went on and on with little noise other than a periodic scream from the courtyard. Mistakes, real and imagined, meant that the man had to begin again at the beginning: *eins, zwei, drei, vier, fünf*, and so on. My teacher showed no outward emotion when this happened and simply rearranged the grains into the original shape. Clearly he was insane.

The monster was a well-read and highly educated man who nonetheless believed in the existence of vampires and other mythological creatures. He believed that by counting rice, he, a Nazi vampire, could not bite. He had told me this truth one morning early in my stay at the prison, at the embryonic stage of my exposure to music. It was a lucid and carefree moment for the vampire.

From the first grain of rice to whatever number his warped mind agreed was correct, the vampire would not attend to me, and that meant for a short while my thoughts were my own. I owned my musings until it was time again to keep his malignant spirit contained. At those times I thought about my Jenny, buried but not dead, and the fun I had dropping rotting pumpkins and wanted posters on the imperious, pompous people back home.

After the final grain had been placed in the dish, he would declare to me that the total was correct and bang the desk with his baton in childlike glee. My teacher would then throw the rice tokens into a wastepaper basket. The food would soon be sold on the prison black market by the guard standing behind my left shoulder.

I remember one of those mornings very clearly. The sound of the rice landing in the trash basket was a signal. I knew what would happen next and kept my body passive as I watched his face drop its veneer of humanity to become, yet again, the bloodsucker of East Berlin and, of course, my personal torturer. When that happened (and it happened often), it was truly a Mr. Hyde metamorphosis, and the transformational bridge from almost human to monster required a payment. I knew it and Alvin, the reluctant Nazi standing behind me, knew it. The only question was, would it be death or just blood? Would it be me or someone else?

The monster, my teacher, glared outside with a hangman's yes, and everyone on the other side of that window scurried out of sight. He turned back to me and pointed to a far corner of the room. "Son, find a line in the wood and trace it across the room." It was to be me that day — I was the bridge.

My eyes were excellent in those wonderful, carefree days; I traced the line on that floor from corner to corner with ease. Where I encountered drops of blood or other body fluids I detoured around them. The monster hovered nearby to ensure accuracy. I had done this before and was beginning to enjoy the experience. No — I was starting to see the *need* for it. I realized that by tracing lines or counting things I could keep myself safe from death.

My music lesson began when I had found the route across the floor, from west to east, and stood upright in my thin prison slippers. I received a condescending nod from my teacher. "My son, pick it up and play."

The ugly, tarnished violin in my hands, I played the prescribed notes and practised techniques for hours. Eventually I had begun to learn complicated new songs based on the notes and themes that had been bashed into me for months. Mistakes were common and the beatings for mistakes were unremitting, as he was a tireless monster. By the middle of the afternoon on that day my head and neck were badly cut and I was cowering with my arms around my head in a corner of the room.

The vampire man stood over my damaged body and ravaged spirit and explained things to me. "I beat you, my boy, to teach you to play just like when you were young. I cannot understand why you have forgotten so much. Sometimes I think I should have hit you more when you were little. Perhaps then I would not have found you with that man's cock in your ass when you were fourteen. Your perversions are against human decency and a disgrace to our family. Sodomy has no place in the Third Reich!" He paused as if trying to clear his mind, then said, "Why? Why? Why?"

I stood and played again. This time I played flawlessly.

As always, the lesson ended at 4:55 p.m. precisely, because the creature was needed at the *potence* by five. I use that word because the death of another always energized the colonel, recharging the monster within. Guard Alvin handed me some of the rice from the trash as I was hustled back to my cell, the old violin held tightly under my left arm. I ate the porridge given to me by a camp sycophant, mixing in the rice, which I had soaked with water from the toilet. I ate and thought about music. In my mind I was home in Pumpkin Town, soaring in my little airplane.

I do not know when I began to play the instrument, but the sounds of its strings began to emulate the movements of my Jenny. The music became beautiful. I realized that a breakthrough had occurred — I could play the instrument with elegance and perfection. I just could. I turned and climbed and descended. I felt the vibrations of the wings and listened to the beautiful little engine as it forced the propeller to dig into the air. I smelled the aviation fuel and the leather seats.

The violin and I were fast becoming friends. As I played, Jenny and I soared together above the treetops and followed the Grand River as it wound its way for miles through the countryside in search of Lake Erie. Once there, just above the water on my Pegasus, we frightened the blue heron feeding on trout and salmon and watched as Canada geese hustled their little ones close to shore, away from the demons lurking below the surface of the water. Then, as the notes went higher and higher, we climbed through and then over the fluffy clouds towards the sun.

I became lost in the wonderful sounds the old violin produced. I was no longer a prisoner waiting to die but a spirit in the wind, flowing with the music. It was the music of chaos and colour and freedom. I should have questioned why I had been allowed a moment of wonder and joy. The wax was melting and I did not notice.

Thinking Cap Again

My guard did not take me to the *Kommandant*'s office the next morning, nor the next or the next. I was fed and allowed to wash but otherwise left alone for days. The time was filled with playing the violin. I did not know it, but the monster had placed a stool near my cell where he sat and listened. I played everything I knew and some music that I'd never heard before, improvising whenever it seemed right to do so. When I put the instrument down, the silence was deafening. It roared down the hallway of the cellblock and stopped at my door, demanding that I play again.

I was beginning to enjoy my new daily routine when one morning I was again brought to the office, where I stood in front of the desk and watched him count his rice. The old routines began anew. For two months I played for the monster, my father, on that beautiful, ugly old piece of wood and glue. It seemed that he appreciated my growing skill, because I was rewarded by not being hit or threatened. Not being abused felt wonderful. I became more complacent and stupid and hopeful, because I had misplaced my thinking helmet for the second time in my life. I had forgotten that I was a prisoner in a madhouse and the victim of an insane torturer.

It was late in the afternoon and I had successfully completed a tricky piece by Bach, the Chaconne from Partita number 2. It is a very challenging piece, with jagged chords that give the music a feeling of great unease and unresolved tension, ending in an unpredictable cacophony of melody and rhythm. As he listened, the monster attempted to drum his fingers along with the tempo and beat, but the music and the rhythm eluded him. My father had been checking a list of names on a page spread in front of him, When the music ended, he jabbed his finger halfway down the list. He grinned, a wolf's smile, and looked at me.

The Folks of No Fixed Address

I am not homeless and never have been. I own the family farm but haven't been there since 1960. It is rented out to a nice German family; my lawyer charges them the cost of the taxes, legal fees, and a small stipend that I receive each Friday in cash. I can't sell it because of something buried there. The farm and the home on it are mine but I cannot live there. When I die, whoever is living there gets the farm, minus one acre. As part of the deal, that acre must be tended carefully. I am a broken guy who can't be part of the scene, as they used to say in the 1960s. Far out, man, is where I am.

Under the bridge where I have my other home, the other residents and I have a couple of understandings. Understanding number one is that everyone steals from each other, and that is why we all carry all our possessions with us always. I use an old grocery cart I stole from a Dominion store parking lot in 1969. My stuff is carefully stored in plastic bins and organized from the shelf at the bottom to about two feet above my head. My important stuff is in a red bin in the middle and an old German Luger, minus the bullets, is secured on top of that red container. Other residents use wagons or packs or just plastic bags.

The second thing we all understand is that nobody can ever trust an alcoholic to do anything they promise to do. I'm not going to tell you why but will let you figure it out. On the other hand, everyone trusts the heroin or cocaine addicts — always. Again, think a bit and you will know why.

A third interesting item is money. All of us always have enough. We beg and panhandle and make about twenty to forty dollars a day. That is not much by the standard of a middle-class person. With most of that money we buy food. With the rest of the money, most purchase something that will give them a bit of chemical amnesia. Some of us have other sources of income, such as welfare, pensions, workers' compensation, and so on.

Finally, I want you to understand that most of us want to be homeless and cannot and could not survive as part of the regular world. Why have I told you these seemingly irrelevant things? C'mon, think. It is because a man like me needs predictability. In prison it was different.

All I have said is true but there is a *but*. Everybody stays away from me because they all know that when my helmet is stashed in my Dominion grocery cart, I am hungry. When the helmet is in my cart, the bikes and plastic bags make way for me. I load my cart very carefully and begin my search.

The American

She was an American. Americans in those days had a certain swagger, a cock-of-the-walk swagger that usually managed to alienate them from the rest of humans. This woman, despite being in a rather dangerous predicament, still managed the posture and strut. It was a full force fuck-you, delivered and signed for by every person watching.

I was playing that stupid German folksong that morning for the colonel. It was a song he often instructed me to play. I was facing the window and he was facing me, signing Nazi things on thick Nazi paper. The American woman was pulled out of a Gestapo car — black, of course — and made to stand in the cold, wearing only the thin striped uniform the Gestapo made people wear after capture. Curly blond hair cascaded down her back and her eyes were partially hidden by bangs at the front. I saw her and she saw me, and we were in love. My playing faltered for a beat; my jailer turned to the window and saw what was happening. He said and did nothing.

Alvin escorted me to my cell that evening, an unusual event. "Forget it," he said and had the guard lock my door. Then he stared through the peephole, shook his head, and said what sounded like "*Nachzehrer.*"

Days later, I was standing beside the camp commander's desk, playing something jaunty. He always had me stand close when he was addressing his child. He stopped my playing and murmured, "Son, over the years I have had you followed, and I think you know why. It's just not natural, what you do. But now that girl . . . I am so happy and relieved, so relieved, my son."

With that my American was ushered into the office. In her hand was a flute that she had smuggled into the prison. That day we played together for my father and he laughed and clapped along with the music.

We played music together for many days after that. The Colonel was happy that his boy had found a girl and that they made sweet music together. He brought his cello to the office one morning and we all played together. Afterwards he smiled and said, "Just like old times, my son. But I do not know you, my dear. Are you a friend of my son? I have never known him to play music with a woman." With that he frowned and waved us out of the room.

That night, my love was brought to my cell by Alvin, and it was obvious that it had not been his idea. He was worried and upset and had forgotten to wear his helmet — that was unusual and should have been a warning. His worry made me worry, and my concern was transported to my American. Nevertheless she entered my cell, closed the door behind her, peeled away her prison costume, and gently slid on top of me.

It was lovemaking and it was fucking to mark the end of time. It was mindful and it was mindless. For our few hours together it was joyous, pleasure times infinity; for a very tiny moment I forgot that I was in a death prison. Before light, Alvin opened the cell door and beckoned for my American to leave. We kissed and held hands and then she was gone. That was the last time I made love to anybody. What happened later destroyed that for me.

At noon I was taken outside and made to stand by the alternative gallows. It was freezing, but I knew this execution was not to be mine when my table and chair were set beside me and the sausage and scrambled eggs were brought from the colonel's kitchen and placed on the table.

Alvin strode out ahead of the *Kommandant*. As he pretended to arrange the plate properly, he whispered in German, "*Verdammter*."

The love of my life, still in the clothing she had worn to my cell, trussed from shoulders to ankles, was carried to the gibbet by two leering guards. I stood and ran towards her, but a soldier hit me on the side of my head with the end of his rifle. I awoke on the ground at the feet of my love as she choked and then died. I lay on the ground forever and watched as she began to sway and sway at the end of that rope, a plaything of the wind.

I watched her, feeling dead myself, as I practised for my father later that day. The egg and sausage and the table were placed just outside the window, between my love and me. Cold snow began to accumulate on the plate.

A Meal of Hangman's Sausage

After a week, a month (I do not know), the colonel spoke of the incident. I was standing to one side of his desk, with a clear view of the empty beams. I would have killed the beast, but I had no strength and no will. The beast knew that and continued the destruction of my humanity.

Quietly he signed a death certificate and then turned it towards me. It had her name at the top, and beside the name it stated "American spy." The monster said, "You pretended to be my dead son to get my affection. You are a liar, a murderer, and so I had her hanged."

For the first time since my stay at the prison, I froze with shock. Tears ran down my face and when I could move again I got to my knees and crawled to my *Vater* and hugged his legs. "I will be your son, I will be him! Just bring her back! Please stop!" I pleaded.

"My son is dead. Look at your arm!"

I did as I was told. I wanted to please my father.

"Read that number, out loud. Shout it!"

I read the number aloud. "Zero nine, zero one, four zero!"

"I was told that you followed my boy all the way to the ground, shooting and shooting, never giving him a chance to bail out or land."

It was true. In my excitement I had overkilled the enemy plane, ensuring the deaths of all trapped in the burning fuselage. I had given it all nine yards. It was during the late afternoon of September 1, 1940.

I could not move, his grip was so severe. He pulled me to my feet. The creature grabbed my chin this time. "Murderer, look me in the eye as I tell you one more thing."

I looked, still trying to please my father, this monster.

"The woman you loved, I know you fucked her. I had her hanged the next day because Dr. Nachzehrer wanted her dead with sperm in her. We give all our dead women to Dr. Nachzehrer. He wanted your woman's ovaries for his experiments, so I obliged him. The second you fucked her, you condemned her to death."

I turned to the table that followed me everywhere like a seductive shadow, and I reached for the china plate located in the middle and ate the festering sausages and mouldy scrambled eggs.

"Sorry, father," I said as I slithered away to my cell, now unescorted.

Later that evening Alvin spoke through the door. "Flying Officer, you are now one of us, the walking dead. You ate the breakfast. You know, of course, that the sausage was not pork and the eggs not from a chicken?"

I nodded and murmured, "I have always known that. I am now not a man but a horror, broken on the wheel."

"I have come to tell you about one of our myths, about a monster — the *Nachzehrer* that the colonel alluded to earlier. You remember? Good. The *Nachzehrer* is an undead creature, like a vampire — but that is not technically correct. *Nachzehrer*s do not suck the blood of the living but instead consume their essence. They are created when someone dies an unnatural death."

I nodded slowly, and he continued. "Do you comprehend what I am saying and what the colonel meant? He knows you are now such a creature, just like him, just like me, just like that doctor who takes our dead women away."

Pumpkin Man

I need a break from my tale of Hell for a few moments. I

feel a very great need to tell a funny story about another thing that happened to the pumpkin man. There is a selection of short stories written by a man named Leacock about a little town in Ontario, near Lake Simcoe. The people in that book seem to have a slightly skewed and ironic outlook on life, as if each day is a little out of focus. Our town of German descent was a little like Leacock's town of Mariposa. For one thing, its name had been changed from a fine German one to the name of a very unsuccessful English general who thought concentration camps for women and children were a good way to win the Boer War. He is one of those forgotten assholes of history, but our forefathers thought it best to name our town after him.

The people from the town named after an asshole became more and more agitated by our silly fly-bys and pumpkin smashes. They had their meetings and made posters and offered rewards, as you know, but they could not catch the elusive Pumpkin Pilot. The good citizens were upset because the orange biplane reminded them of World War I attack aircraft from Germany. My Jenny was made in either the U.S.A. or Canada and was briefly used by our side from 1917 to 1918, but anger and facts seldom mix.

They had a difficult time, during the six months of meetings at City Hall, deciding on a name for their committee and then making a plan to catch the Pumpkin Pilot. After much debate and compromise, they decided to call themselves the Airplane Search Supervisors. It was an unfortunate acronym, but it stuck — they were the ASS men. The committee was angry that they were called the ASS men but they could not change the name because the citizens loved it. Besides, it would have taken even more meetings and heated debate to change things and the summer holidays had started.

The ASS men decided that a Saturday in June was the day to begin the search. A large map of the town and surrounding farms was taped to the dirty window of the Five and Dime. Strange orange crayon lines were very carefully drawn on the map from the centre of town outward towards recent sightings. I was there that Saturday, as indignant as the others and ready to do my part to catch the guy causing the orange ruckus.

The men gathered downtown formed teams of two, and each team was given a section of the map to search. We got into our cars or tractors or onto our horses and began to ride the roads and knock on doors. My team eventually arrived at our farm, where my dad met us with his old bolt-action rifle in his arms. Jennifer was parked about four hundred yards away in the middle of her runway, as orange as any pumpkin can be. She was obviously an orange airplane.

My partner, the city mayor himself and head ass, started a conversation with my dad that he clearly did not want to have.

"So, Karl, what's that orange contraption way out yonder in that field, then?"

My dad looked carefully in that direction. Using his left hand to shade his eyes from the morning sun, he accidentally pointed his Mauser Gewehr 88 at the pre-eminent ass with his right. "Why, Wolfgang, that's a tractor."

The ASS boss was puzzled and said, "But Karl, it's orange, and tractors are never orange."

Dad looked at Wolfgang and said, "Well, I've seen your tractor and it's green and yellow, so why can't mine be orange?"

"Orange?"

"Yah."

"Looks like an airplane — an orange one at that."

"Nope. It's my tractor, painted orange to keep the gophers away."

"Groundhogs, you say?"

"Ground squirrels. Did I say groundhogs? I meant squirrels. They hate the colour orange because it reminds them of pumpkins, and everybody knows that pumpkin seeds kill gophers, er, groundhogs. No chipmunks means no burrows, which means no more holes in the ground. You got that, Wolf?"

"Looks like a plane, though."

"No, it's a tractor."

"What's that long strip of land in the middle of the corn for, then?"

"Wolf, I thought that would be obvious to a scientific thinker such as yourself. It's my practice area to scare gophers. That's why my tractor is sitting there, in the practice area. Einstein, from Germany, it's his idea. It's all relative, you understand?"

"Yup, makes sense."

Within a month, every farmer north of the city named after a man who liked concentration camps had orange tractors to scare away the rabbits. It was scientific, they said, like the guy who invented gravity.

I decided to use the Latin I had learned in Grade 12 and created a new name for the mayor's club: "Pumpkin Observations Over *Perpetuum*."

Eating

It doesn't take any effort at all to take *essentia* juice from people who have been spewing their innards for years. The alcoholic who has lost everything to Mother Gin, the crack addict with no teeth and a face that has endured constant itching and picking, the schizophrenic, the depressed, the heroin addict furiously pedalling her bicycle to her dealer and back. Then there are the sad ones, eating their doughnuts and sipping their over-sugared coffee at the shop with the striped awnings. They all feed me. Yes, they all quench my need to instill misery in others — unless, of course, I keep that helmet over my head.

A truth: I despise being a sucker of souls. I believe that means I still possess a tiny sliver of humanity. Not much, but enough to have a friend like the man witnessing my life story.

When I am unable to control my need, I venture out of my box and sit somewhere near people and then carefully remove my metal busby. I scan the coffee shop or look at the people sharing the underpass with me and eventually I find that person. I move close and say something that will begin the downward slide. I wait for a certain response and then I feed, and sometimes I take so much that they die. It is disgusting. I hate those bastards who gave me the vampire bite that day when they killed her, the day I ate the breakfast.

A Violin and a Coin

Another truth: Do not ever truly wish for something unless you understand that every gift has a dark side, a flipside, like the tails on a coin. Not an ordinary coin, mind you, but the *Totenkopf* coin, the SS coin, the schilling skull coin.

After I broke and ate the savage food I was no longer invited to play for the commander of the prison. His unwillingness to further taunt and hurt convinced me that he had gotten what he wanted. That was, of course, revenge against the naive young pilot who was too stupid to stop firing bullets at a doomed Henkel HE 111 as it plunged in a steep spiral towards the farmland of England.

Alone in the darkness of my cell, I began to hallucinate. I became the *Kommandant*'s son in that aircraft as it spun and spun, unable to escape, spinning closer and closer, seeing the surprised look on the face of a man tilling a field as the noise and spinning terrified his farm animals. Yes, the *Oberstleutnant* had been successful. I was broken and had become his son and experienced full force the terror of impending death, at the gallows and in the cockpit. Our father was a genius.

Other times in my cell, alone and cold, I was relieved that the torture had stopped. But I was wrong about that, because the torture had not stopped. The quiet in my cell, the silence of the tomb, was only recess. Final classes were about to begin.

The *Oberstleutnant*, our father, met me at my cell days, weeks, centuries later. I think that he wanted to bury his son, because he had the violin with him, safely stored in an old, battered leather case. He was gentle as he handed me the instrument.

I understood then that in the vast universe there are many different instruments of torture and that each has its own vibrations and echoes. I imagine the iron maiden singing a lovely melody as its door swings inwards on rusting hinges and the prisoner inside gets the point. I took the violin and hugged it to my chest because I had grown to love it and, in some ways, love that man, my father, my destroyer. I nodded my thanks.

He stared at me for a long moment and then at the violin. He said, "My son is dead, and you killed him. You are my son, and I have killed you." He stood at the cell door, swaying back and forth, for a long time, lost somewhere.

The violin was merely a thing made from dark brown

wood and it was ugly because it had been thoroughly soaked in the juice of the tortured and the damned. I think both of us, the sons of the monster, could claim that to be true. I should have smashed it on the floor, but I kept it because I loved it. I knew, deep in what was left of my soul, that taking, accepting, and loving the gift from the monster was eating more of the eggs and sausage.

I played and played as my father had intended, sending music throughout that place, unhappy, melancholy sounds, for days and days, until the Russian army arrived. As I played I began to detect the essence of others. I recognized it as the misery and despair of those waiting in the prison and the staff waiting with them. It was sweet-tasting and it was disgusting. It was only a small whiff, a tiny beginning, and I loved it. I played and played, the sounds inviting the juice of human suffering to enter my cell and then penetrate my skull and lodge in a dark place that had not existed until the monster, my father, had created it. My *Vater* was indeed a genius.

I did not sleep anymore. I played until my damaged hands could not bear the pressure of the strings, and then I screamed and screamed and screamed. I screamed until the hurt in my fingertips disappeared, and then I played until the pain returned. It was the start of my transformation from human to monster. The violin provided the energy, the lightning for this Kafkaesque metamorphosis, and the monster within opened an eye.

Dr. Frankenstein had awakened me, but it would take a letter and coal and grit and dark places for the monster to fully exist.

To Exist

Only the truly happy are immune to my hunger, like my friend the teacher. When I first began my panhandler/soul-sucker career in the 1950s, most people walked about with their heads held high, talking and laughing, looking about and making eye contact with each other. Meals were a little harder to get back then. Now, in 2018, most people are anxious and stressed, with their heads oriented downwards, with their eyes digitally attached to tiny computers that seem to exert control over mind and body. I believe that machines have finally taken over the world. I feed on their despair and longing as they stare vacuously into the machine void and wait and wait for someone — anyone — to acknowledge their existence. They are the dispossessed, trailing their essence behind them like the smell from a rotting carcass.

Russian Efficiency

The Russians were hours away and I wanted Alvin to escape. He had not been particularly kind but he had not been unkind. His rare moments of humour and disrespect towards his commander had become my only joy, tiny but there, in an overwhelming pit of darkness and anxiety.

The Soviet advance into Berlin created panic among the prison staff, but the pricks remained Nazi until the end. In one twenty-four-hour period they executed 120 prisoners via assembly line, using all three appliances. I knew that some who were about to be released had been murdered by accident. Those poor souls screamed their innocence until the end. The bodies were piled neatly along the length of the north wall, opposite the main gate. Job complete, some of the guards and staff then scurried away.

The prison was eerily silent as three people hunkered down in the main office: Alvin, the *Oberstleutnant*, and me. Alvin sat behind the desk. I was in Alvin's usual place at the door. The former chief executioner was standing between us, in my usual place. We were waiting for five p.m., but I was worried for Alvin.

"Alvin, take a car or something and get the hell out of here." I handed him a note that I hoped would help him in the trials ahead. I didn't think so, but a chance is a chance, and the man deserved a chance.

Alvin shook his head and took a long puff on a stale cigarette he had pilfered from the top drawer of the desk. He exhaled the smoke as he spoke, ensuring that most of it enveloped the former leader of the prison. "No, Flying Officer Paine. I am a doomed man. The Russians will execute me when they arrive or the British will give me a fair trial and then hang me. When the British noose descends over my head, I will wish that I had taken the Soviet offering. They are, above all else, a practical people. I fear that soon they will take our place as purveyors of terror. Tell your leaders to place a metal wall around them. No, pilot Paine, I will stay and see some justice done for you before the Red Army takes my life away."

It was four-thirty in the afternoon. I watched Alvin smoke that cigarette until it burned his fingertips and remembered what he had told me about metal hats the evening before, after we had stormed the Warden's office and forced him to stand at attention all night, waiting for the Red Army to arrive. "RAF man, have you ever seen me at this camp without this metal helmet on my fat German head?"

I told him no, or once maybe.

"Right. Do you know why?"

I shrugged.

"I hate this heavy, badly designed helmet. It looks like the knob end of a penis, and while some would say I'm a true dickhead, this helmet is a terrible thing to wear all day."

I smiled for the first time in months and replied, "Protection of some sort, I presume, or you just like to pretend to be a Nazi." We had dressed in our respective uniforms and brushed our hair and looked very spit-and-polish.

"This is an army helmet, not a Nazi helmet. But protection, yes. Yes, protection." Alvin looked out the window and sighed. He shook his head sadly and said, "Gary, horror and despair — true horror and despair — are everywhere, but at this place, more than any other place, that juice is squeezed and squeezed and wrung from the doomed every day. It is thick and juicy here, like a good steak." Alvin was explaining this in a tone that did not invite debate. He made a circling motion with his hands and cut the pretend meat with a pretend knife. "I have tasted this evil fluid and it is intoxicating and heady, better than the best of wines and more exciting than a beautiful woman in heat. The helmet protects me from becoming addicted to that putrescent gumbo. I have wanted not to need the juice — the violence, the despair, the cruelty — to live, and neither should you, despite what has happened at this place. Yet I fear it is too late for you, that you have already tasted."

I thought about what he said as the former *Oberstleutnant* continued to stand between us, trussed and ready to be cooked, rocking back and forth and mumbling about his dead son and something about a scarlet letter. "Okay" was all I said, because it sounded like mumbo-jumbo, hocus-pocus, and abracadabra all being boiled together in one diabolist pot. But yes, I had had a taste.

Alvin was not finished. He handed me a pair of World War I aviation goggles and said, "There is more. There are ghouls and vile creatures that will now seek you out. They are a higher order of the damned and feed on creatures such as me, you, and him. Those things can smell the crap that we eat. You cannot see them unless you wear the goggles. I have seen them."

Alvin stood up. "I hear the Soviet tanks at the front gate, so we must hurry, my enemy and my friend. First, take a little more advice from a crazy lawyer, and it is this: pilot man, you have been broken on the wheel of misfortune and, I fear, will never recover. I know this and you know this. When you return to your world, you will not fit in anymore. You will live on the fringe of your world forever, always watching and never participating."

He removed his metal talisman and tossed it to me. Its weight was almost unbearable, and it seemed to burn my fingers. "Wear this, if you can bear its mass. It will keep the juice from drowning you. The good German steel may save you, but I think not. Wear the goggles to see the others coming. Now let us take this man to his execution. It is almost five o'clock."

We marched the former commander of the prison to the death room and made him strip and fold his clothes neatly and place them on the bench. We shoved him to the death house and placed him on a stool below the same meat hook that had killed my friend. I was wearing Alvin's helmet when I looped the noose around his neck. There was no hood, because I wanted him to see what was coming and I needed to watch his eyes as he died.

Alvin attached the other end of the rope to the shining, newly cleaned steel projection suspended from the ceiling. I reached into my pocket and removed an uncooked German sausage and an egg. I opened his mouth and stuffed both under his tongue. Then we walked to the middle of the room, drank some schnapps, and waited.

Freedom?

Three Russian infantry soldiers leaped through the door, weapons raised. They shot Private Alvin on sight and shook my hand after I screamed that I was English. They offered, and I accepted, some vodka from a flask. When they saw the former commander of the prison under the hook with a noose around his neck, they seemed perplexed, and shrugged. I sat at my desk drinking Russian spirits as they pushed my violin teacher from his perch. I still love the casual efficiency of that gesture. I removed my new hat and watched the dancing man until he was still. The taste of his despair was wonderful.

"Are you Paine?" a Soviet major asked me as the camp commander completed his tango. He told me that a beautiful woman, a partisan, Ona Krasivaya, was waiting for me outside the front gate. They said she was asking for me by name and for someone named MacDonald.

I thanked the soldier for freeing me and ran from the death house to the front of the prison, where the gate had been torn down by a heavy Soviet tank. The machine sat idling in the centre of the compound, its machine gun about to execute the prison guards who were being shuffled into a crowd where one wall of the courtyard mct another. Some were begging for their life, but most stood calmly, waiting for the gift of large-calibre bullets. I noticed the man who had beaten a frail prisoner so badly that he vomited onto the cold pavement. I tapped the Russian officer on the shoulder and pointed. The Russian soldiers immediately pulled aside the German and nailed him upside down on the gibbet that had killed my American. Russians are so damned efficient.

I remember the noise of the machine gun as I embraced Lorraine. It was one of those living metaphors that are both bitter and sweet at the same time. Lorraine took my hands into her hands and asked, "Mac?"

"Dead," I said.

She nodded and said, "Walk with me, Paine. We will drink some wine and we will talk."

We walked through the streets of Berlin together until we found a café that was open, despite the Russian invasion. We found a small table next to a dirt-streaked window, so we could watch the Red Army roll down the street as they searched for enemy snipers.

Lorraine sipped her wine, grimaced at the bitter taste, and finally asked, "When? How? Do not lie or make it easy on me, Gary. I need to know. He was my stupid, brilliant, loving husband and he was the father of our little girl." Lorraine had been a vicious partisan whom the Nazis had named the Cutter, but now she was a grieving wife and mother. There was much pain in her eyes as she spoke, and I told her everything.

I told the woman how they had hanged her man as I watched from my chair and table, and how for a few moments I had shared in his suffering. I described how he had lived on the end of that hook for thirty minutes before he was still. I repeated the few words we had traded before they took us to the killing room. I explained that I had puked over that table when he was dead.

Then I unburdened my own sorrow — how I was a broken man because I had loved for a few days and then, for a second time, had watched helplessly as they had tortured and then killed someone I loved. She did not try to soothe my sorrow or give advice. She knew now what I had become.

As we finished the bottle she spoke more about her husband. Lorraine told me that MacDonald had been a Rhodes Scholar and was studying corporate law in Paris in 1935, when they met and married. In May 1937 they had a child and they named her Lily, after the beautiful yellow flowers that grew wild in the meadow near their cottage. His French was excellent and he could tell a good joke in either language. Mac had known that the Nazis were coming, so in early 1939 he had returned to Canada and trained at a place he referred to only as Camp X.

Then Lorraine told me about their daughter, Lily. They had made love in a field of those beautiful yellow wildflowers while she was being made. She and Mac had danced and sipped wine and eaten a lunch of cheese and bread and made love again. Lily was born the following May, and the child was a joy to all who knew her. Just after her third birthday the Nazi army marched through France on their way to Dunkirk. A small group of soldiers stopped by the house where Lily and Lorraine lived, waiting for Mac to return from Canada. The soldiers demanded wine and food and sex. She refused and tried to escape with Lily, but they took the child and threw her against an ancient stone wall. She had died screaming for her mother to help her. The soldiers then turned their attention to Lorraine, now unencumbered by her child.

Lorraine poured the last of the wine into my glass and looked at me. She told me that Mac had loved me because I made him laugh with my stories about flying pumpkins and falling pilots. Mac had told Lorraine that our trip and the fun we had on the *Empress of Britain* had been like a holiday from worry and fear. MacDonald had been very happy when he arrived in England, knowing that he had made a good friend.

She took my hand and we walked back to the prison gates. I held Lorraine in my arms for a long time, thinking about their little house and the fields of beautiful lilies growing wild and brilliant in the sun. I saw rainclouds cover that sun and bring darkness to the image, and I held that precious woman closer. I whispered, "I am so sorry," as I let her go.

Lorraine smiled at me and nodded towards the prison. She asked me to describe its layout, especially the location of the building and the exact hook where Mac had died. She thanked me for loving her husband and for making him laugh. I asked her what she was going to do.

"Why, Mr. Paine, I am going to die. I have nothing to live for anymore." She walked away from me then, through the gates of the prison and into the death room.

I waited for her all night outside the prison gates, but she did not return. I walked from that place with the name I wish not to repeat and did not look back, because perhaps ghouls would be watching. "Goodbye, my good friends. Goodbye, my American," I said.

Prince Edward Island Potatoes

Is it a wonder that I question whether my experiences — as I remember them, as I tell them — are real? Is it a wonder that I sometimes wonder if my memories are a mere figment of a piece of undercooked Prince Edward Island potato? It all seems real; I see the physical scars on my face and body and feel the trauma that cuts keenly through the centre my spirit. My dad, the one who raised me from birth until I left for England and who had frightened the POOP Committee president, would have said that it doesn't matter. But it matters very much to me.

The ghouls that search for me are real. Do I know this to be true? They are real, aren't they? I watch for them every day with my X-ray glasses, because they have found me before. The bastards rent and chewed that time. Yes, I saw them. Yes, I saw them eat my pals, but they didn't get me. Hmm. Then again, perhaps my friend sitting across from me right this minute, as I dictate my story, is only a chimera, pretending to listen and scribe for me every Saturday morning with coffee in one hand and raisin muffin crumbs on his lap. But I can see him on his cement block, and I see clearly the HP computer that sometimes causes him frustration and anger. I believe, I believe!

I have one foot stepping in the shit of reality and the other foot in a world where the ghouls live, and it takes a pair of magic goggles to see them coming. I believe they are real. Real. Real. Real. I must not let them get me and complete the work that insane man started in that place that shall remain unnamed. I live under a bridge in a box because I must — there is no other way for me. I must always watch, always watch, always watch, watch always for the ghouls that took my friends on the bridge where a young American woman told me not to jump. I must remember to look for things that are real like that ghost woman.

She was a young old woman. She used to walk through our cardboard town every morning, heading north, and each night she would return and head through our camp, heading straight south. She had been making the trip forever, it seemed. You knew she had arrived by her quiet singing, always the same German folksong, over and over. It was music that nobody other than I recognized. The woman wore an old black dress, faded but in good repair. She did not look at anyone as she passed, and nobody openly acknowledged her for a long time. I found her presence somewhat irritating and I was happier when she was gone, either north or south. Others told me they felt the same way. They were afraid as I was afraid.

One morning, on a whim and with helmet and goggles firmly in their place, I wished the lady in the black dress a good morning as she passed my home. I was drinking coffee and eating a doughnut. She stopped and turned my way.

She was terrifyingly beautiful and then terrifyingly ugly. She was my coin. She was the coin I had been given and then thrown away. One word escaped from her mouth: "Alone." She took my coffee, turned to the north, and went to whatever she did during the day.

That evening I waited for the coin to return, and she did not disappoint me. She wore a red dress this time and she was holding the hand of a child of about two years of age. I am poor at guessing age; the child could have been older. The woman walked past my spot under the bridge and claimed her own area. In time she had her own box and plastic and blankets.

"Thank you for seeing me," she said. "I thought I was invisible. I wondered if I was a ghost."

England-Bound

One night can make a difference. It sounds like a cliché, but it is true. That morning as I walked away from the prison after waiting all night for Lorraine, things were different. I had known when she walked through the gates that I would never see Madame Cutter of Nazi Balls again. We all had choices to make that day, I suppose.

I watched the Russian soldiers — and I use the word *soldier* very loosely, because they had become a rabble overnight as I waited for Mac's wife. The soldiers were also making choices and decisions: to kill or not to kill, rape or not to rape, steal or not to steal. I sound like fucking Shakespeare, and I am truly sorry, but I tried to decide whether I was witnessing a comedy or a tragedy. An entire family — mother, husband, and children — shot because they didn't leave their home fast enough was certainly a tragic event for the family, but the situation unfolding before me had elements of a classic comedy or farce. Somebody laughed like an idiot and someone else screamed something in Russian, and I decided that it was a comedy. Two days before, even the day before, as Lorraine and I sipped our wine, civil order had been alive and well, but twenty-four hours later it was vaudeville. The comedians were the drunk soldiers and their unwilling shills, the ordinary Germans. They danced and cried together.

A sane person would run from such a place, but I chose to stay in the Russian part of Berlin for a month. I began to feel almost human as I watched and listened from the bell tower of an ancient church, once home to a dead German sniper. The show wound its way through the various acts. In the end, after a month, it was over. The deafening applause of silence roared up and down the streets, over the bodies and the bricks and the trash. Even the crying of the women and girls had stopped. *Time to go*, I thought, because I was beginning to feel shitty again.

It is about a thousand kilometres from Berlin, Germany, to Calais, France, or about six hundred miles. I had not experienced fresh air or open space for almost four years, so I decided to walk home. My uniform made the trip easy enough. I ran through Germany and sauntered through Belgium and France. I was fed and sheltered by the advancing armies of the United States and Great Britain once I had told them my story. I walked, hoping to free myself from the horrible anxiety that death-row inmates feel every day, especially the ones who have no clue when the rope is coming.

It was raining heavily one afternoon as I approached Calais, so I put on the goggles to keep the water out of my eyes. I was surprised to see that I was being followed by the strangest-looking people I had ever seen, even in prison. I removed the glasses, shook my head, and looked around for a few minutes. "Very strange," I remember muttering to myself, and continued my journey.

It was the late summer of 1945 and it was harvest time. I remembered my Jenny and the great pumpkin drop-and-smash of 1936. I was a destroyed man, wondering if my Jenny could revive me. I thought that it might be possible, despite everything. I knew that I would never be okay again and likely not lead a normal life, but there was Jenny waiting for me in Pumpkin Town.

My plan was to board a ship in Calais and, once in England, report to the War Office, collect my medals, and receive a hero's welcome and the acknowledgement due a Battle of Britain fighter-pilot ace. Perhaps they would offer to help with the blackness of despair that had descended upon my spirit. Perhaps the doctors could give me a pill or something.

Calais had taken a beating while our troops waited for deliverance on the beach at Dunkirk in 1940. The remnants of that destruction were still evident in August 1945, when I arrived. It was a busy port, as the import-export business between Britain and Europe was slowly resuming.

I noticed British troops boarding a destroyer. I reported to the duty officer whose job was to deal with misplaced British soldiers. He had me wait in a small room; the door was locked. In time a blanket and mattress were brought to me and some food and water. In the morning I was shocked when the military police arrived, placed me in shackles, and escorted me to a waiting airplane. I was flown directly to London. Nobody spoke and nobody looked at me.

The Scarlet Letter

The letter must have passed through many hands before it landed on the desk of the great Sholto Douglas. He would have then sent it directly back down the chain of command for appropriate consideration. Because of that letter, I was arrested by the military police upon setting foot on English soil.

I was placed on a kind of house arrest, fed twice a day, and given a warm, comfortable room. None of my queries were acknowledged and I was mostly ignored. After a few weeks I found myself in a dank room under the Royal Air Force headquarters. Despite the stark surroundings and the grim looks from the only other person in the room, I was optimistic that my terrible experiences in East Berlin were about to be acknowledged. A thick file dominated the left-hand side of his desk and a single piece of paper sat bestride the middle. A fireplace was lazily burning coal in the corner of the room.

I stood on another X, this one invisible. The man began: "Mr. Paine, I am not a military man but a civilian lawyer. The military has washed its hands of you, and so we meet in this basement room. This pile to my left contains all the records of your training and military career, but we will get to those in a moment." He glanced briefly towards the fireplace and sniffed.

The lawyer looked at the single paper in front of him but did not touch it. He said, "This letter is from Kommandant Ralph Vater in Germany. I'm certain that you know this kind and compassionate man. He has asked us not to hang you as a traitor." The man looked at me with venom and hate.

I was shocked. Compassion was not a thing any Nazi understood. "But he hanged and tortured — " was all I had time to say.

The man at the desk screamed, "Shut up, you fucking traitor!" Then, in his lawyer voice, he read the letter:

April 1, 1945

Sholto Douglas
Air Chief Marshall
RAF Fighter Command
Royal Air Force
London, England

Dear Sir,

I hope that you are well in these trying times between our two countries.

This letter has been smuggled to you directly from my hands at a civilian prison in Berlin. Before this war wends its way to its inevitable conclusion, and before we release one of our prisoners back to England, I wish to describe for you the behaviour and conduct of Flying Officer Gerard Kurt Paine.

As you will know, Royal Air Force pilot Paine was shot down over occupied France in the fall of 1940 and captured by the SS. There was confusion at the time of Paine's arrest. The SS, assuming him to be a spy, accidentally transported Paine to this prison in East Berlin. I would have immediately arranged to have the young man taken to the appropriate prisoner-of-war compound but for his unpatriotic and cowardly behaviour. In short, this man shared with us information on aircraft specifi-cations and various military installations, in the hope of special treatment. Because of this, we deemed it appropriate to incarcerate pilot Paine for the duration of the war at a prison more suited for traitors and spies. I am certain you agree. He will, however, be released upon the secession of military hostilities.

I beg you to allow ex–Royal Air Force pilot Paine, when he returns to England, to remain unpunished for his actions, as he is a despondent and broken man and poses no further threat to England or the Commonwealth. May I suggest further that Paine merely be stripped of his rank and that all documents pertaining to his involvement with the Royal Air Force and the war be destroyed. I believe a fitting conclusion to this distasteful episode would be to make him invisible, as if he had never existed.

I beg of you one favour. Attached is a small package that I ask to be given to Paine as he leaves for home. I would be very much obliged to you, sir, if this small thing could be accomplished. It is a token that will have meaning for him.

I wish you well in the coming years of peace.

Your humble servant,
Kommandant Vater
Strafgefängnis Plötzensee Prison
Berlin, Germany

I noticed a dark seal at the bottom of the letter and that the signature was in red ink. My father, my teacher, my persecutor had played his endgame. I was the walking dead.

The civilian lawyer handed me a small envelope that had been opened and resealed. Then he looked over my shoulder to the door. He said quietly, "The real reason that you are not being hanged is because you shot down thirteen enemy aircraft during the battle for Britain. Instead you will be taken from here to a ship bound for Canada."

With that he took my file and my life and burned them in the fireplace. He did not destroy the letter from my father. Then he turned to me again and sneered, "Change into civilian clothing, return to this room, and burn your RAF uniform."

In an adjoining room a shirt and tie and brown pants awaited. After changing, I returned to the room and tossed a bundle of rags into that fire. As my prison clothes burned I was escorted in handcuffs from the building into a waiting car and then driven to the port of Southampton. Then I was quickly put on an old steamship bound for Montreal, Canada. I took on board with me a large suitcase with my treasures.

I opened the envelope while sitting on my bunk deep in the viscera of that ship. A small coin spilled out and fell onto the floor. It was a Nazi schilling, minted in 1933, with a soaring eagle on one side and a grinning skull on the other. I understood its meaning immediately, my *Vater*'s intention. Life — the eagle, a daydream of the forlorn — had been granted, but it was a fool's comfort, given by a monster to his plaything. The skull side offered other things.

Spins with Jenny

In time I became a cocky bastard wannabe pilot. On the other hand, perhaps I was already a cocksure maladroit asshole, before I found my winged hag. I'm not sure. For certain I was young and impulsive and loved life's challenges, even the ones that could kill.

After a time of trial and error and then success, I understood that landing was landing, and that trying to land while watching cows eat grass in a field where they had no business being was a bad idea. On those occasions when my mind wandered, I would forget to make the corrections in speed and rudder control to stay lined up with the runway. Jenny was a temperamental lady who demanded full attention to her parts — otherwise, *bumpety-bump*.

Turning was turning and climbing was climbing, though at first I saw those as two separate manoeuvres. I could turn the Jenny by coordinating the ailerons and rudder. I could also climb the Jenny quite well. It was hard work, and I wondered more than once why the person who had designed my winged beast hadn't made the aircraft more naturally stable. An hour or two of flying that airplane exhausted me and my brain would be jelly.

I could climb or I could turn, but, as I have explained, I had not tried to climb while turning. One beautiful sunny afternoon I decided to do both together, at the same time. At three thousand feet above the ground I applied full throttle and yanked the stick into my stomach, and we climbed. We slowed quite a bit, but that was nothing unusual. In a moment of impulse I moved the stick to the left — too far — and pressed the rudder bar on the left — too much. Poor Jenny shook, and suddenly her right wing dropped like a rock. We were upside down for a second and then we began to spin to the right, towards the ground.

I had absolutely, positively no idea what to do as we twisted in that flat spin towards the earth. It was as if the horizon was moving around me and I was frozen in space. I freed my hands and feet from the controls and began to count the revolutions, hoping that the turns would stop on their own. I screamed out the count: *One, two, three, four, five* complete rotations, and nothing changed. If anything, they had become faster and the ground was coming towards me like a demon vortex. There was loud whimpering and crying in the cockpit when I heard the Jenny speak to me.

"It's fine, Gary, my love. I know what to do," she said in the sexiest voice I had ever heard.

"Jenny?" I asked. "You can talk?"

I heard a laugh, and suddenly the power went to neutral and the stick went completely forward. I screamed, "No, no! Bad idea!" It seemed suicidal to quicken our journey down to our death, plus take away the power.

"It's fine, darling," Jenny crooned. Then I felt the rudder pedal move all the way to the left. The spinning stopped and we were in a steep dive. The stick came into my stomach and Jenny climbed out of the dive. Full power again and we climbed back to three thousand feet. "Almost there, my sweets," Jenny said. We levelled off and the power was reduced.

"Oh my god!" I cried, either because I was shocked that my airplane had talked or because I knew that I would live. I'm still not certain. Both? I suppose it does not matter.

Then my airplane said," Now, my sweets, that we are safe and sound, can you take me home? I'm a bit sleepy. Is that smell coming from your pants?"

A truth: Airplanes can speak.

Another: Do not turn sharply while in a steep climb.

A third: To spin is fun, unless it kills you.

A question: Can airplanes speak?

Jenny and I spun and spun all over the countryside as she taught me how to dance.

Coal

The *Empress of Britain* had taken MacDonald and me to England from Canada in June of 1939. Now that wonderful ship lay on the bottom of the ocean, just off the coast of Ireland, having been torpedoed twice by a German U-boat. It was the same beautiful ship that had returned the King to London. My inglorious return to Canada was a different kind of trip.

It was a freighter, a working ship returning to Montreal, that was my home as I returned to Canada. This time Mac wasn't there to play games and pranks with and talk about the future. Mac was dead. His wife was dead. My American was dead. I contemplated the nature of fate and chance as that sluggish ship steamed its way across the cold Atlantic.

It was not a free and easy passage to Montreal that I had been given. My berth, as I said, was well below the waterline, and my job was to shovel coal to keep the fires going, off and on for twelve hours a day for eight days. It was considered the lowest work on the ship. That was fine, because deep in the bowels of that freighter, as I toiled along with the other lost men, the other eye opened. I began to taste and enjoy the despair that those men reeked of, like terrible farts. My brain sniffed and I ate. The food was delicious, and its effects took away my own malaise and horror and despair.

My helmet and uniform were stored carefully in my locker as I lurched through my work periods and off times. A whisper here and a question there pushed despondent men deeper into despair. I consumed what they spilled, and I was happy. To an older man struggling to keep up with the younger workers I said, "Boy, we are the lowest of the low in this boat, with no chance of better things. Time goes by so slowly." To a sad young man making his first voyage I murmured, "I hear you left a wife back home in the care of your best friend. I bet you miss her. Don't worry, you can always trust a friend."

An old-timer who looked ill was trying to sleep in the bunk above mine when I said, "That cough sounds serious. You should get it checked, because it could be cancer. I had a cousin once with a cough like that and he was dead within weeks of that first cough." To an addicted gambler I whispered, "That's a lot of money you lost, and you were saying you have bills to pay at home."

As I spread the seeds of worry and anxiety throughout the coal room, production and the ship's speed slowed. Yelling and berating from our foreman added to the growing dysfunction of our tiny piece of the ship — as you may know, dysfunction and despair are first cousins. And then one day I tried too hard and I killed. My intention had not been murder, but murder it was.

It started innocently enough. "So why are you working in this shit job, my friend?" I asked a worker covered in coal dust, still bent over after a prolonged coughing spell. He looked my way and said nothing. *Perfect*, I thought. *People with nothing to say always have plenty to say.*

"Where are you from?" I asked. It was an easy question — most people know where they are from.

The man straightened up and wiped coal slime from his eyes and answered, "London, England."

I asked, "You were in London during the Blitz?"

The man nodded and said, with little pride, "I was a fireman during that time."

I knew that his despair would be mine. Most men who had battled the blazes during the Blitz were proud of their actions during that terrible time. This man seemed embarrassed and upset. "How bad was it, my friend? How bad were the burning hot destructive flames?" I asked.

The man looked upwards, through the ship and back to the fires and chaos of the bombing of London. "They were bad. Thousands of bombs rained down on London from December 1940 on. Thousands and thousands, and I didn't think we would ever get the flames out. Some of my mates went into a building and it toppled on them. I heard a few quick screams and then only the fury of the flames.

As they died I was holding a hose that drew water from the Thames, two miles away. All bloody night I held that bloody hose, and all the next bloody day. Ice and black, evil soot became my world. I thought the world was ending, and I wondered if we could defeat a nation that would do that to our people."

"Yes, I saw those flames from above, and it seemed like Armageddon," I said.

"I remember morning arriving and the fire was less furious. Citizens began to arrive to search for loved ones or help in any way they could. I was relieved for a few hours and went home for some sleep. I woke up at twelve and had a couple of beers and then fell asleep again." The man stopped talking and looked towards the floor.

Almost feeding time, I thought. *Almost. Just one or two more questions and it's all mine.* "So, what happened?" I said, as sympathetically as I could. I put my hand gently on his shoulder.

"Oh my god, oh my god! I failed to awaken in time for my return to the fire station at three p.m. I missed the call to go."

"Where in London was the call?" Another simple question intended to deepen his despair and obvious self-loathing. It was almost harvest time.

The man started to sweat, another sign that I was getting somewhere, and he said, "Near the Guards' Chapel, Birdcage Walk — near Westminster, near the palace. Why?"

I waited for a few shovelfuls because our foreman was on the prowl. "Just asking. I'm a Canadian and I spent most of the war as a prisoner in Berlin, after being shot down." This admission always loosened tongues.

"Do you know about the chapel at all?" he asked as he leaned on his heavy, blackened steel shovel.

I scratched my filthy hair for a few moments and pretended to search my memory, "Ah, sure I do. A V-1 or V-2 rocket hit there and destroyed the place and killed some people. Am I correct?" I asked, the man, who was now visibly upset as I showed as much care and concern as possible without being stupidly dramatic. I was famished and getting hungrier, and the lamb was ready.

"Yes, people died," he said, and tears began to stream down his face, mixing with the filth from the coal dust.

Then I pounced and grabbed as much humanity as I could before it fled screaming about the ship. I asked him, "You seem upset about it. Why? I think I read somewhere that a London fireman didn't show up to help with the fire and people perished. He was drunk or something like that. That wasn't you, of course."

The man stared at me, threw his shovel at the approaching foreman — hitting him in the head — ran up the winding stairs to the main deck, and jumped into the Atlantic Ocean. The foreman died as well. I was promoted to foreman for the final three days of the voyage, because I was seen trying to help the man. The helmet stayed in the locker.

From 1946 until 1959 I worked in the bowels of that ship as the head coal-stoker and part-time mechanic. I refused every offer of promotion that would have enabled me to climb out of the bottom of that oceangoing transport ship. The smells and the dirt suited me and my desires. The metal of that rusty old ship was my incubator, my womb, my cocoon, as I completed my transformation into an inhuman monster. Covered in tar and coal and engine grease I prowled about in the bowels and entrails of that ship and found the most horrible places, places where only rats and other foul creatures would dare venture. In those foul places, I hated, and I became what I am today.

I hated my German father who had killed me, and I hated the Royal Air Force for believing that bastard's letter and then condemning me to nothingness. I hated myself. I became the monster. I am still the monster. I roared and roared as I paced and paced, causing the rats to scurry away in fear and wonder. As I ate, I destroyed. Below decks I ate until there was nothing left to consume, and I became a creature among hollow men. Then I looked upwards.

It was said that at night a monster stalked the upper decks and that the creature was as black as coal tar, and as it passed it farted sadness and despair. The higher decks became my larder because, down the cold metal stairs, the hollow men now avoided me. I had to eat, after all, and I discovered that even those not tarnished by the darkness of the coal and the gloom had something to give. It was one of those eureka moments when I realized that everyone — anyone, anywhere — could be made weary and forlorn enough to give me what I needed. The chief engineer was worried that his wife was alone in England. The steward for the captain was a drinker. All those who prepared meals for the passengers and crew hated their work. The stowaway passengers and the prostitutes who were hidden here and there were furtive and nervous all the time. The first officer was dying from cancer and wanted to be home.

In June 1959 we docked in Montreal, Canada, and it was the first time I had stepped off that ship in thirteen years. The ship would be in port for a week, so I booked a room in town. I had a shower and looked at myself in a full-length mirror. The dirt was gone and the prison scars marked my face and body in crazy, chaotic patterns. Embedded in my chest was a perfectly formed devil's head, a permanent tattoo in coal ink. That beautiful black head seemed to be grinning.

I did not return to the ship and watched gleefully as it

left port, bound for New York. I picked up my stuff from under the hotel bed and the monster, fully formed, headed home.

Prison Terror and Stalking Demons

PTSD. "Prison terror and stalking demons" is what I call it, and it was the reason I could not live at home on the farm. Why? Simple, really, and I will explain. In June 1959 I went home and tried to be okay, sane, my parents' child, a citizen of Pumpkin-Smash Town. My parents did not ask about the war or about the puckered scar around my neck or about the tar that clung to my skin. They did not ask why it had taken me so long to come back to the farm.

They did not ask, and their eyes told me that they did not recognize the monster that had stepped off the bus at the country-road intersection near the farm. My dad was old. He shook my hand, loaded my two things into the trunk of his Ford, and drove me home. Mom was old too. She made an excellent meal of ham, corn, scalloped potatoes, and, of course, apple pie and real ice cream. Nobody talked. The silence was horrible, and deeply disturbing to us all. I was a monster licking the ice cream from my fork and my parents were old and did not know how to help me.

My dad refused my help with the afternoon chores, so I wandered here and there. Of course I ended up sitting between four oak trees and four rocks. I spoke with Jenny, and she answered me.

"Hey, babe, I see that you waited for me," I said to the ground between the trees.

I was shocked when she answered, "I do not know you, sir. You are a stranger to me."

"It's me, Gary," I replied and waited.

Jenny laughed and said, "You are not Gary. You look like Gary, but you are not he."

"Why do you say that? You are mine. I stole you and flew you. We're pumpkin-smashing mates," I replied to my Jenny, who was beneath me in bits and pieces, wrapped in oilskin tarps, six feet beneath my feet.

"What are you?" she asked instead of answering my question.

That was a question I had been wrestling with since leaving the prison arm in arm with MacDonald's wife, but by then I knew the answer. I was a soul-sucking, dog-ass, juice-drinking monster. Or perhaps I was just a broken man who had dived into schizophrenia to preserve whatever humanity was left inside. I said nothing to Jenny.

The minutes went by, and then Jenny said, "The Warden, your other father, told me to expect you."

"Me, Gary?"

"No, Gary is dead. I told you that. His memories are with me. We were the pumpkin crew."

"Then who am I?"

"You are not a who. You are a what."

"What am I, then?"

"Monster. You are a monster. Your dad from Germany told me that he killed Gary and you killed your dad's only son. He said that you murdered him. And, monster, you killed my kind thirteen times."

I scrabbled with my ungues to unearth Jenny, to make her whole again and have things the way they used to be. The earth would not cooperate, and I stopped digging. "But Jenny, you are mine. I loved you."

"No. I belonged to Gary Kurt Paine and he was a fun-loving, innocent boy. I loved him as soon as I saw him standing in line for a ride. I killed the pilot so that we could be together forever. It was me that landed us in that field and missed the tree. Leave me here. Leave us here. Monster, you have no place in this world. You can look in at the world, monster, but you can never be a part of it. You can't and I can't. You drink the juice of sadness to live. Wear the helmet and the goggles, monster. Leave us alone. Go... go... go."

I stood up and saw my father watching from ten feet away. He hesitated, searching for the right noun. "Young man, who were you talking with just now?"

"Jenny. And Dad?"

My dad folded his arms in front of his chest and said, "Yes." It was not a question but a statement.

I asked the man who was one of my fathers, "Am I crazy or did Jenny speak from under here?" I pointed to a spot on the ground.

"Does it matter," he asked. Again it was more a statement than a question.

"No, I guess not," I whispered.

The man who I loved, my dad, was crying. He grabbed my shoulders and pulled me into his chest and said, "Go from here and do not return until we are gone. Leave Jenny be."

Yellow Pencils

I was not depressed or particularly sad. It was life fatigue. It was an awareness that for the remainder of my days I would itch for, lust after, and solicit the essence of the dispossessed and anxious. I knew that I was a user of others, and that when you take from others, they become less and have less. I had become a malignant spirit and I had no way to stop other than through death. And so I took my helmet and goggles and suitcase to Niagara Falls to end me. If you have been listening — er, I mean paying attention to my story so far, you will know why I chose a bridge that connected Canada and the United States of America.

That same train that took me to Toronto in 1939, when I tricked the conductor, took me to Toronto again in late 1959, and then on to the city of Niagara Falls. I paid my fare this time, from the money my dad had given me the day he told me to leave the farm and let Jenny rest in pieces. I had the ticket ready for the man with the official Canadian National Railway hat, but he walked by me without saying a word. It was the same man as before.

I stepped off the train and into the train station in the bustling city of Niagara Falls, with a dirty duffel bag containing my clothes and the helmet and goggles that had been given to me by the camp guard. So far I had not used them because I did not believe in magic or ghosts. A black suitcase containing something wrapped carefully in tissue paper was my other possession. I lugged both items towards the bridge that spanned the chasm between the United States and Canada.

At the apex of the bridge I stopped a moment before jumping, because a small school group was approaching, enjoying the experience of straddling two countries. Their clothes seemed a bit old-fashioned, but I decided that was a trick of the light. They spoke with the veterans who were sitting at the west end of the span, selling pencils. Many of the ex-soldiers were missing limbs but were happy about the attention given them by the children. The children did their best to help, buying all the pencils that were for sale.

I dropped my Nazi schilling from the bridge and counted to five before it struck the frigid twirling waters of the Niagara River. Considering the number five for a minute, I wondered what would flash through my mind during my own five-second plunge downward, until the impact with the water or my drowning ended my cravings. I wondered which side of the coin had hit the water first.

An eleven-year-old girl with T-strap shoes and a navy dress and hat stopped beside me to drop her own coin, and together we timed its descent. It took her nickel ten seconds until it disappeared and presumably sank to the bottom. Time for the girl and time for me were distinctly different that day. The girl laughed and turned to me and said, "Don't jump, Gary. There are better ways. I love you. I will always love you." She skipped over to her classmates as they walked home to the United States. With her first step into the United States, she turned her head, smiled, and then disappeared.

When I stepped back from the edge of the bridge a twinkling caught my eye. The shining came from a small opening at the bottom of the escarpment, on the American side of the Falls. I made my way across the bridge and down to the bottom of the escarpment and squeezed inside. Light from other openings, cracks and crevices, was sending streams of colour and brilliance into a very large cave with offshoots and tunnels. My head suddenly cleared. I realized that ice — thick ice, a cave of ice — could be the perfect place to keep at bay certain ugly needs and to hide from ghouls.

At night I stayed in my crystal palace with thick blankets around me. After saluting the former King of England, I drank gin until I fell asleep. In the morning, when the sun rose high enough to light the interior of my haven, I would clamber up the escarpment and join my brothers on the bridge. I would sit on a small stool next to Farewell and Shaky, two veterans from the war that had killed me and had killed them and every man begging along that bridge.

The inevitable hangover would be my other companion until noon. Noon was my time for crying.

Sometimes I ask older citizens if they remember the legless, armless, useless veterans who sat along that bridge selling pencils, and the answer is always no. That is very strange, because I remember that thousands of people walked by our honour guard, year after year, smiling and laughing and looking forward to some shopping in the United States. Some gave us money and got a pencil in return and then pretended not to look at the stumps and other injuries. If they were observant they would have seen something in our eyes, something malevolent. We were watching them.

Here is a question: How do you feel after seeing and perhaps talking with the lost and forgotten? "Bad" is the answer, I expect. We do that as we take from you what you have. We feel better as you feel worse, and that is the essence of the vampire bite.

Remembering Dad

My father — the father who ran our farm in Kitchener — was a quiet and reflective man and I loved him. I knew him as Dad or Pop and I remember him to be a fair parent and very protective of his family. He did not raise his voice and he never hit or hurt either my mother or me. He demonstrated his love through actions and deeds. You will hopefully recall the time the POOP president arrived at our house and the way my father protected his impulsive son.

Nights were bad for this wonderful man. His screams created a cone of silence around our home as the crickets and frogs stopped to listen to the strange loud noise coming from a place between the meadow and the pond. As a child

I waited until the insects and other creatures began their hullabaloo again, as a signal that Dad was finally at peace. His screams often included a name: Wilhelm.

When I was told by my father to leave the farm and leave Jenny buried forever, he handed me three letters. I tucked them away and did not read them until I was safely hidden in the ice cave. The first of the three letters had my name on it. The paper was smooth and unwrinkled and the writing was in German.

Meine Bube,

I am writing this letter on the day I met you and will give it and the other two letters to you when you are twenty years older. When that day arrives, I will buy you a drink, hand you the letters, and get drunk with my boy/man.

The other letters were written by me to my mother while I was overseas during the Great War. They are the only ones I wrote during those terrible years and they were never mailed, as I was fighting for the Germans. You will wonder how a Canadian farm boy ended up fighting against his friends and countrymen. It's a long story, but I will make it brief.

I was born in Germany in 1892 in a small town near the French border called Baden-Baden, very near the Black Forest. When I was five or six, our family immigrated to Berlin, Ontario, Canada, and bought this farm with money my parents had saved and borrowed. In 1913 I returned to Germany to visit our relatives to pay back the borrowed money and to visit the warm springs my parents had often talked about as they worked about the land.

The Great War happened, and presto, I was a private soldier fighting in the trenches against friends and countrymen. To my knowledge I did not hurt or kill a fellow Canadian, because I aimed high, but you never know where a bullet will go after it leaves the muzzle of a gun. I did, however, kill a German. Please read the other letters and you will understand what I mean.

Love,
Your father

The second letter was dated August 1916 and was written by my dad to his mother.

My dearest mother,

Well, I still live, and that is a wonder considering the circumstances that I find myself in. I will not describe, Mother, the mud and water and disease, but I will speak of humanity. Germans, English, Canadians, French, Scottish — we are just men, all the same, and we all want the same things. Of those things the most sought-after and the most valued is friendship. Mind you, strong drink and warm food come a very close second and third.

Sometimes late at night, when our officers are sleeping somewhere behind the front lines, we speak with the enemy, I as translator. We exchange stories of home, people we love and miss, and if we are very careful we trade good German sausages for decent French wine. You see, Mother, we are just young men who want and need the same things. We do not understand economics or politics and do not care if the other side gains or loses 100 yards of mud and water or owns a stupid hill overlooking more mud.

At home I have few friends and no true close friend. Mother, you know that I am a loner who would rather hitch up a team and plow a field than go to town. But here in the mud I have made a true and great friend. He watches my back and I watch his. My friend's name is Wilhelm. We share food and drink, and at night one of us is always awake. I am quiet and he is loud. I am a farm boy and he is from Munich and attended university there. He is married and I am merely engaged. He likes coffee and I like strong tea. Wilhelm loves German lager and I like Canadian rye whisky. He is a German patriot and I am not, but sitting in a hellhole with a machine gun between us, we are comrades in the true sense of the word.

By the way, Mother, I have tried to keep my feet dry and my hands clean, as you always tell me, but alas, the putrid water of our trench and the lack of soap have made this a challenge.

Your ever-loving son,
Karl

My father's final letter, dated August 1917, was different.

Mother,

I am writing this letter quickly because it is sunrise and I and 11 other ordinary private soldiers have been detailed to execute my friend Wilhelm by firing squad. He will die by the hands of his friends because he hid in our trench as the Canadians attacked. His nervous system just could not take it any longer. Christ, he was with me at Ypres and the Somme and then at Arras.

It is here at Passchendaele, fighting the Canadians, that he snapped. Christ, oh Christ, this man won the Iron Cross second-class during the Battle of the Somme. Mother, it is insane that they will extinguish such a man.

Wilhelm would have been fine if he had told the officer who found him that he had slipped or something, but as always he told the truth, and now he will die by my bullet or by another's. I will not miss, because I do not want him to suffer. I never miss.

Shit, I must go. They are calling for me and I see my friend being marched to his final place. He will be bound to a chair and a blindfold will be placed over his eyes. I'm glad about that, because I do not want my friend to see me. I am so glad that I gave him a quart to drink last night, and so perhaps he will not be aware.

This is my last letter, Mother. When this stupid war ends, I will make my way home, work the farm, and be a good man. I promise this to you. I hope that Margaret is still waiting for me.

Margaret, of course, was my mother.

Shaky and Farewell

Farewell sat to my right and Shaky to my left. We sat together all day selling pencils to people walking from the Canadian side of the bridge to the American side. I had a seller's permit in my back pocket. The American vets had responsibility for the opposite side. They had a depressing despondent look, and I'm sure we were the mirror image.

Shaky shook all day, but I was told that when he slept, he was calm and serene. Shaky had been a corporal with the Royal Winnipeg Rifles of the Third Canadian Infantry Division when they stormed Juno Beach on June 6, 1944. He was in the first wave and was certain he had been the first soldier to step onto the sand that morning. Shaky had been very frightened as he made his way forward, realizing that he might perish that day. Friends beside him were blown apart or shot dead. Others lost limbs or eyes or ears as he crawled, hunkered down, crawled some more, and then finally stopped when he realized that the German gunners could not see him anymore. He told me that he had turned around and watched as more and more soldiers poured onto Juno Beach. When the beach was full, they pushed forward, but delay after delay cost lives and limbs. Shaky was fine; he worked hard to keep his small platoon on the move towards the railway line that was their objective.

Shaky could not hold a cup of coffee and shook even when he walked. Nobody laughed or teased our friend, because we would not let that happen. I asked him about his shakes and why he was sitting on that freakshow bridge with Farewell, me, and the others.

"I'm at the bridge for the same reason you are and Farewell is."

"Okay, then, why are we here at this place?"

"Easy. We want them to suffer as we suffer. It makes us feel better when they feel terrible. I'm right and you know it."

Yes, I knew it. "Why do you shake? What the hell happened?"

"Okay, remember I was telling you about June sixth and the railway line we were to capture?"

"Yes."

"Well, I led my men straight to the station, about a mile from the beach, and nothing happened. No Germans and no civilians, just us."

"Sounds peaceful."

"It was, until . . ."

We waited for our mate to continue, but he could not. Shaky never did tell us about that day except to say that the next night he was shipped back to England, and that his shakes have continued since that day at the rail line near Juno Beach.

Our other friend, Farewell, was happy to tell his tale again and again. We always listened. His was a story of loss. Farewell had no arms below the shoulders. We called him Farewell after the novel by that guy who liked fish.

Our guy, like the guy in the story, had lost his arms, his gun, and the love of his life. While chasing enemy soldiers, Farewell had rounded a corner in a small town in France and was confronted by "Hitler's buzzsaw," an MG 42 machine gun. The bullets took his arms and the head of the man running behind him. His name had been Shorty. The soldier behind Shorty was lucky and lost only an ear.

We existed like that until September 1977 — Shaky, Farewell, and I. It was a life of sorts. We fed a bit, sold a few yellow pencils, and talked. At night I relied on the thick ice to help me drink my gin, and during the day I was a vampire. Like I said, it was a life of sorts, but sometimes a person has no idea when something is about to end.

At night the ice cave kept me safe from the monsters and ghouls. It had not occurred to me during those months and months to explore the hollow ice cube beyond the front area where I tried to sleep. I'd had a headache all day, and that night the beautiful frozen thickness of the place did not take it away. Mother Gin stared at me from her usual place near the cave entrance, offering something I could not take for the moment. On a whim, or perhaps because of a moment of clarity and saneness, I decided to go exploring.

I had plenty of stolen flashlights, so I began my grand adventure. The main tunnel was beautiful, with sheer walls of glistening ice that, strangely, were weeping long strings of water from the ceiling to the floor. I licked the surface for a moment and the tears tasted like age. I laughed, of course, but for the first time in many years I had that anxious stomach ache where moths and other things flutter about. You know what I mean.

It was weird, but I recognized the entrance to the first room as soon as I came upon it — a small opening at knee height. It was possible to stand up after I entered the space.

The flashlight kindled beautiful ice bubbles and cracks in the ceiling and the walls. There too, tears dropped and stained the walls on their journey to the floor. I traced a large drop to the floor and then froze when I saw what littered the place. It wasn't elephant bones that covered the floor but something far stranger, and horrifying. No, elephant bones would not have shocked me, and even John Merrick's remains would have gotten only a chuckle. Christ, I was living across the river from Clifton Hill, home to wax vampires and world records, after all.

I was astonished to see that every inch of the floor was covered with carefully constructed and exquisitely painted tiny plastic models of German aircraft, in groups of thirteen: ME 109s and 110s, Henkel and Dornier bombers, and of course Stuka dive bombers. I picked up a perfect Henkel 111 and saw . . . something in the bomber.

I crawled out of that place and back to the main tunnel, then examined other rooms, other spaces. They were the same. Bombers and fighters were lined up ready for takeoff in a strange, cold miniature world. It couldn't have been me who glued together and painted those things, I thought. Could it? I decided to ask Farewell and Shaky about it the next day on the bridge as we sold pencils to tourists.

It was the end of the summer holidays and the bridge traffic was slow. I decided to reorganize my bag and suitcase and then cleaned the pilot glasses with a piece of discarded tissue. Pointing to my ice hideout, I was just about to describe the plastic models and weeping ice when Farewell suddenly yelped and gagged and began to swing his stumps about as if he were fighting something. Next to him, Shaky stopped shaking. Across the way, the Americans seemed to be dealing with something terrible as well. I could see nothing except one or two late-season tourists making their way from Canada to where we sat at the apex of the bridge. Farewell shrieked again and then dove cleanly over the railing of the bridge, down to the river. I didn't hear a splash. Shaky had disappeared as well.

The Nazi guard had told me that my goggles would make things — terrible things — appear, and I had not believed him. I put the goggles over my head and slid them quickly over my eyes, and then I believed him. Creatures — ghouls, five of them — were all around us, biting and devouring my companions. They slithered on all four limbs. They had red, weeping eyes that did not blink, and they were very thin, like malnourished snakes. They did not speak or make any noise of any kind. It occurred to me as I watched the others being consumed that those monsters were merely harvesting their cattle after they had been fattened and made stupid on the bridge. They were vicious and methodical, and they wore torn and bloody German air force uniforms.

I jumped up and down and gestured at the mayhem and slaughter before me. I ran to a customs booth on the Canadian side and screamed, "Look, look! My friends are being eaten by horrible creatures! Please do something! You have a gun — shoot them!"

The man came out of his booth and stared up the slope of the bridge to where it began to slide towards the United States. He shook his head and said, "Nobody there, pal, except them two tourists staring at you. Calm down."

I screamed again. "The ghouls — look, they're tearing my friends to pieces! Look!"

The guard got angry and grabbed me by the shoulders and said, "Gary, I know you. I've known you for a long time. You've been selling pencils here for years, but there's nobody else. You've had this bridge to yourself for a long time. You talk to yourself all day long, and that's fine, but stop yelling and scaring people." He pushed me away from the booth area and shook his head.

There was a church spire a mile away and I ran for that landmark, certain that the monsters and ghouls were inches behind me. At the door I hesitated because, in my mind, in my form of religion, God was an asshole. Or, like I said before, she was a god that cared shit about people, especially the brave ones. Therefore I had no expectations when I banged on the great wooden door at the front. The door was locked, and nobody answered my frantic pleas for admittance.

I glanced quickly behind and to the left and right and saw only tourists having nervous breakdowns. I spoke to the absent landlady looking down at me from above the door of the church, like a gargoyle. "Well, I guess ghosts and ghouls and monsters just can't run. But I can run, and run I will."

I ran home to New Berlin.

Pumpkin City

By 1970 I was back in the city formerly known as New Berlin, the pumpkin-smashing capital of the world. Huge shopping malls were the rage, and large highways and roads all eventually led to those ridiculous buildings. Homeless communities had sprung up downtown and under bridges near the shopping centres. I had my place under one of those bridges, staking out my spot near a path that led to Fairway Road. I used my goggles quite a bit to look for the ghouls that had murdered my friends Farewell and Shaky. The helmet was used to ensure that I did not indulge too much in the insipid. For a long time I was a very contented creature.

A homeless person can make some real money as a

violin-playing panhandler if he or she can play. I can play. No, I can play well. My violin creates twirling sound-waves that are often too sublime for the human mind to understand. I learned to play the instrument despite and because of threatened and real violence to my body and to my mind. Pain and hurt created in me the very finest violin player in the world. I have heard the others play on records, on the eight-track and four-track cassettes, I think they were called, the CDs, the MP3 *Star Wars* things, and iPod earplugs. Some players are excellent, but I am the best because my skills were annealed in a prison of anxiety, torture, despair, and bloody, horrible death. I play as the devil plays while the ghouls dance. No, I do not play for money. I play for myself, and for my friend MacDonald, and for my American. I play for all the men and women who did not leave that horrible place.

The years flashed by and then it was 1978, and a newer and bigger cardboard box under the bridge was my place. Until that September day in 1978, I was just another homeless panhandler, but one with a terrible secret — a hunger that I have hopefully described for you quite well.

It was the car that attracted my attention that morning forty-one years ago. I had started my shift at seven a.m. on the northwest corner of King Street and Fairway Road. Cars could not make a right turn on a red light, so it was a perfect place to talk with drivers and perhaps feed. I had my helmet firmly perched on my head and the pilot goggles were hanging around my neck (just in case), but it was talk and a laugh I was craving that morning — I was bored. The car was red and fast and looked brand, spanking new. The top was down and the very young man driving the red Mustang had long brown hair and a Steve Prefon-taine moustache. I saw a teacher-type briefcase sitting next to his coffee Thermos in the shotgun seat. I could see that he wanted to make the illegal right turn and risk a ticket, so I leaned onto the side of his car and started to talk. I was not looking for a friend that day, because my last great friend had perished as I watched and did nothing, but I found one.

Before I spoke, I undid the strap under my chin. I asked a question and the young teacher drove around the corner (at the green light) into a hotel parking lot, then walked back to the corner where I was waiting. I have wondered these forty-plus years why he did it, but at that moment we formed a human bond that would comfort me. I say *comfort*, not *cure*, as my disease was too far gone by then to hope for a quick fix. I would still feed on the desperation of the world, but this man, part lunkhead and part virtuoso, would give me something very simple, a thing that everyone, even a beast such as me, wants and needs. Do you know what that simple thing is? No? Yes? Perhaps? That young teacher in his stupid sportscar, which he could not afford unless he was living with his parents, gave me something to look forward to each day. I did not need his money, but I took it. I did not need his sympathy, and he never gave it. He gave me fifteen minutes every weekday morning. I took that, and in time I craved it more than I craved my food.

Suddenly I was ninety-eight years old and the teacher was sixty-two and it was 2017 — exactly one year ago. He still had that stupid red car and he had accumulated a wife, children, grandchildren, and bigger responsibilities at work. In other words he had become a very busy man, but a person who continued to stop every morning at the corner of King and Fairway and talk with me. He is my friend and I trust him. On that day, one year ago, I told him I was ready to die and asked him to write my story. For the past fifty-two Saturday mornings he has listened until noon, he has typed on his old computer, and he has edited, and now my story is almost finished. There is but one more thing I must do, one more terrible thing I must confess to the teacher before my end. I lacked the courage to talk about it before; I do not want to see the man's face when he realizes what I actually am.

I hope that my story will be believed, because it's all true. A few times I was fuzzy about the dates and times, but I did my best. For example, I cannot remember if my beautiful American died at noon or at five like everyone else, but I remember the sun shining above her head as I looked up and into her eyes that day. Oh my god, I am ready to die and perhaps see her again. I wish that She, our god, would return to our cruel world and grant me this small wish. She has been gone for so long, so long, our absent lady of the land.

One error in judgment as a young man cast me into a spiral of pain and despair. What would life have been like had I stayed home and tended the farm with my dad? We would have laughed and cried and harvested the corn every year. I would have met someone and married and had children who would in time take the farm from my arthritic hands. The Curtiss Jenny and I would have flown together for years, moving together like old lovers. And yet perhaps ... perhaps I was meant to be there at that fucking place where great people came to die. Maybe I was there to love my American woman, to give her a bit of pleasure and grace in her last moments and to look into her beautiful blue eyes as her life fled for the unknown, perhaps to have a cross word with God. My American was so beautiful and so American.

Grateful is not the right word to describe how I feel about that naive young Canadian teacher who stopped that day and allowed me into his life. He gave me five dollars that first day and I knew it was all the money he had on him. He went without lunch because a homeless man with a helmet and stupid goggles had asked him a question. I realized then that, despite the trials of my life, there are good and kind people left in the world. Funny that it took me all these years to understand that fact. He listened and wrote my story, and like I said earlier, it is true. That there are no records of my life does not make it less true, and perhaps, in a strange way, it makes it the truest kind of story. Written-down things are sometimes bullshit, as you know, and perhaps that is why I waited until the end to have my friend the history teacher be my witness and scribe.

Okay, I am ready to confess the thing that is missing from my story, and that thing is called "extermination." The teacher can add or not add my confession to my sad chronicle, as he sees fit.

Time is a commodity that each person owns and uses as they see fit (thank you, Captain Obvious). For forty years I have lived under the same bridge and now I count my life in hours and minutes and seconds. Well, from seven until seven-fifteen or so each morning I met the teacher at the corner of King Street and Fairway Road and drank a slightly cooled double-double and ate two double-chocolate doughnuts that he provided along with a five-dollar bill. This simple ceremony has been the highlight of every day for a long time, and I crammed as much into the fifteen minutes as possible. I asked the man about his work and his growing family; he would inquire about the important stuff I had learned from recent issues of the Coffee News. "Good stuff," I would say, laughing. "Interesting and relevant information," I would add. I would explain that cats can't taste sweetness or that a left-handed screwdriver can be used by right-handed people or that dinosaurs still exist.

The teacher would giggle and snort at those stupid tidbits and then roar off in that silly pony Mustang. And sometimes we would talk about other things.

After finishing the coffee and doughnuts, I would panhandle until the morning rush-hour traffic was over and the lanes were dominated by huge cars driven by retired men with silly caps perched on balding heads and city buses driven by dead-eyed city workers. I might tilt back my hat and sniff a bit — nothing much, but it is a pleasurable activity, best done on a rainy day. Around nine-thirty I might return to my home and settle into my box for the day or I might push my cart downtown and watch the world go by. I liked the exercise. You've seen me, I'm sure, pushing my heavy cart down King and up Weber, wearing my helmet and goggles. I was the tall, once handsome, slightly scarred gentleman in the tattered, washed-out uniform.

Sometimes I would have a second double-double at that doughnut place downtown, near the school. It was there that I would catch up on important coffee news. By midafternoon I'd be home with the headphone things I found in a dumpster behind that audio store, rocking and bopping to the young brothers from Australia. A few months ago the Coffee News said that Maurice had died, and I was thunderstruck.

I have not slept properly since 1940, because monsters don't need much sleep. A quick nap in the afternoon when AC/DC "Back in Black" is done seems to be enough rest for me. I know that if I sleep longer than sixty minutes the ghouls will get me and finish me, like they did to my bridge mates. I am desperately afraid of the ghouls and what they will do to me.

At night I watch over the teacher's house. I watch for them — the creatures with Nazi uniforms and the others

— because they know about the teacher. They know where he and his family live, because I have watched them as they walk by the house, pause for a moment to look in the front window, and then walk on. I let them see me and they lurch towards me with outstretched arms and teeth gnashing, as silent, well, as the night. I lead them a merry chase away from the house to downtown, where they belong. Remember, they will not run, as it is not their nature to hurry and because they have all the time in the world.

In the iron ship where I was a member of the black gang of coal-stokers, I killed two innocent people, and in a weird way I was also responsible for the deaths of Private Alvin and my friend Mac and his wife. I executed my Nazi father and perhaps I killed Farewell and Shaky too, because I did not believe in the magic of the goggles.

Teacher, my great and dear friend, I want you to know that I murder still. This need has increased during my stay under the bridge in Pumpkin Town, but I kill only those who need to be killed. I kill them because they are dispensable and will never be missed. I kill assholes because they remind me of that monster in that place. It is from these useless cowards that I get my greatest feeds. These are the meals that keep me alive and feeling almost normal — although I admit that the concept of normal is difficult now for me to grasp. Okay, I'll try again. The big meals take away my depression and my intense feeling of being lost and forsaken in a world where ghouls hunt me and people despise me. They are the nourishment that keeps me alive, while the smaller sniffs that I take between meals are just snacks. It is so very difficult to pass by despair sitting on a bench, waiting for the bus, and not take a sample. It is delicious, much like a double-chocolate doughnut and a large coffee with double cream and double sugar.

My last murder was six months ago and has sustained me until now. When that juice is gone, I will die. Timing is everything in this; I need to get to that death place by noon tomorrow. Here is what happened on that afternoon six months ago.

Of course I had my favourite reading material spread out on the plastic table at the back corner of my favourite red-striped coffee shop. They walked in and ordered the most expensive drink possible, a cold cappa-chia something, and sat in the middle of the place, facing me. One of them was the leader and the other the sycophant. The leader looked at me and commented loudly about the homeless who pollute the streets of Pumpkin Town, and his follower of course snickered and cackled his complete agreement. Their behaviour made other customers nervous and uncomfortable, but it did not bother me. It aroused me. By their second icy cappa cup they were louder with pseudo-dynamism. Other patrons looked towards me with pity and at the assholes with disgust. A wonderful young woman who was enjoying a coffee and a toasted BLT sandwich told them to shut up. I shook my head at her and smiled that it was all right.

The grin was still on my face when I stopped at their table. When I had their attention, I said, "You two are chickenshit assholes who have no future, so today is all about murder. *Death*."

They looked at the goggles covering my eyes and then the helmet that I had placed carefully on the table beside their coffee cups. Both had the furrowed brows that the stupid get when they are trying desperately to understand what is happening.

They followed me when I left the shop, unable now to do anything else. They swaggered down the aisle and tried to make eye contact with other coffee people, but the people had gone and ghouls sat in their places, watching. I think ghouls appreciate a good murder and leave me be while I kill.

I was going to extinguish one or both of those vermin. What would the prison guards have called it? Eradication? No. Liquidation? No. Christ, I can't remember the fucking word, and I had it a few minutes ago.

The men followed me out the side door and into an alley. The ghouls slowly followed in a perfect doughnut line and waited. My victims were silent as they stood in their own very short doughnut line, beginning to leak despair. I could smell and taste their *bête noir* as I stood before them. It was delicious and I wanted to kill, much like my father had wanted to kill his son and me, back then at that place where she died.

The victims tried to recoup some lost courage. "Christ, he smells," the leader said. A stupid, insipid laugh followed this stupid statement.

"Sure does. Needs soap," replied the sidekick.

I was tired and thought for a moment about my friend the teacher. I love truth, but I lied when I said to him that the goggles were broken. I have been able to see the monsters and ghouls since I ran away from the Falls, and I saw them forty years ago, when I flew around the parking lot shooting pretend bullets to scatter them. Ghouls prefer straight lines and hate circles, which confuse them. I see them still; there are thousands and thousands walking in straight lines and making sharp corners in Pumpkin Town. I cannot escape and I am tired of always watching, besides I also hate circles.

At this point I took out my German gun, walked slowly at ghoul-speed over to the Commander, placed it in his stomach, and pulled the trigger. It went *click*. The beast's pathetic negative essence bled from him into me, almost filling the void within me. I knew that if I walked away, the thing before me would live a life of sorts. But I stayed, and I'm certain that the ghouls nodded in unison behind me. I watched as the colonel's body arched and his mouth went wide, as if in orgasm. His eyes popped, and the goo smeared his cheeks much as the ice tears had done in my cave at Niagara Falls. Then he went limp and was as dead as a properly hanged man. It felt glorious. I was eighteen years old again, flying in my Jenny and dropping orange globs on the fine people of New Berlin. I howled and the ghouls danced, albeit very slowly. I danced with them; the song "Sweet Child of Mine" by Guns & Roses, screamed in my mind for some reason.

Oh yes, the other guy. I had almost forgotten about him. He had witnessed the whole thing, so I had a problem. I did not require his essence, but he had seen what he had seen. I wrapped my talons around his head and withdrew enough essence to cause brain damage. I laughed as the thing walked away, likely to join the crazy and homeless, possibly to live in a box under a bridge. I vomited his despair onto the filthy sidewalk as the ghouls followed the newly made hollow man down King Street.

I will die tomorrow at the death house. I want to die, as I am truly tired of living. It has become too much to bear. I do not know what will happen; I fear I will be taken and rendered by the ghouls. If so, it may be a blessing and I will truly be gone, but I hope for better things.

Teacher, I am so sorry that I'm more a monster than a man. I had to tell you. The need to kill is real. Sometimes as I sit in my box, I have wondered if the ghouls are the good guys trying to rid the world of me, a beast, or if they are the ghosts of people I once knew, trying to take me home — but I am certain that this has already occurred to you. I love you, my teacher friend, because in you I have found an honest man who will tell my story honestly.

Hospice Death House

It's Saturday and I have written this addendum quickly as I wait for my friend at the corner where we first met, so that he can drive me to the hospice. I want to give him two things before I enter the death-house prison doors. I will never see my friend again after those gates close behind me. I hope he arrives soon, because I can feel a crowd of ghouls closing in on me to take me away.

Do I hear her calling me? Does she wait for me at that horrible place, and will I play for her a sweet melody of love if we meet again? If our god has listened to this desperate and tortured soul, she will grant me time to play that Cohen song for my American, the one that I have grown to love.

My friend approaches in his old red car and I am ready.

Funeral

Mary and I arrived for Gary's funeral at four p.m., armed with two large blue containers, a steel World War II German army helmet, and a well-used, deeply scratched pair of old flying goggles. The helmet was placed on the cement block on which I had spent quite a bit of time in the past year as I listened and typed. The goggles were strapped around a large, head-shaped piece of quartz that Gary had often held on his lap as he talked. The blue recycling boxes, stuffed with thousands of five-dollar bills, were positioned carefully at the entrance to the bridge cathedral, one at each of the two main pillars. The final items that Mary and I brought to the place were a large double-double from the red-striped coffee shop and a box of double-chocolate doughnuts. Those we kept nearby, just in case our friend showed up.

At 4:30 my school's music teacher arrived with his violin. He smiled when he saw our preparations and we talked briefly. I reminded him that at five p.m. he was to play one song and only one. He knew this already, but I was nervous, and when I'm nervous and anxious, I'm liable to micromanage everybody nearby (my wife hates this about me). When I had completed my instructions to the teacher, Mary told me to chillax. I chillaxed by eating one of the doughnuts in two bites.

At 4:55 — a significant time of day in the former life of our friend — the three of us stood by the helmet and stared at the blue boxes. At 4:59 a young woman stepped into the heartland of the place with a child in tow. Her dress was red and the child looked scared. The woman took the coffee and gave a doughnut to her child. They stood beside Mary and me and we waited.

At 5:01 — hanging time — nothing had changed. I nodded, and my colleague played a sad German folksong without sharps or flats. When he was finished, he carefully placed the violin in a plastic case with our school's name on the front, smiled at me, took a doughnut, and left. When he reached the pillars of the church, he reached into the blue box on the right and took a five-dollar bill, which he tucked carefully into his wallet.

At 5:30 we were still alone. Five-thirty was when the people at the prison usually died, so we waited. I was startled when, from under the bridge, a breath of cold air slowly moved over and around us, stopped and stayed. We waited, but nothing further happened. The air had cooled and my teeth were chattering, despite my fall jacket.

It was 5:45 when I decided to pick up the X-ray glasses. I looked at my wife and she shrugged and then nodded. I put them over my balding head and slid them over my eyes.

I am not going to tell you if I did or did not see anything that afternoon. I am not going to say that I saw ghouls waiting in long doughnut lines, dressed in striped pajamas, staring not at us but at the helmet and goggles. I will not admit that a young man in an old military uniform, holding a young woman's hand, touched the plastic goggles on my head, or admit is that an old soldier tapped lovingly on the dick hat. What I will tell is that when we left that home-less village, only two Canadian five-dollar bills remained in each of the bins. Mary and I took one five-dollar bill each and the mother and child picked up the others.

I will not say whether Gary whispered something in my ear or what he may have said. If I admit those things it means that I am insane, or that Gary's story was the truth and creatures such as those do exist. After all, how can a story told from a place of torture and despair be the unal-tered truth. Does it matter?

Goodbye, My Friend

The second-last thing Gerald did before we left to go to the hospice was hand me a very large Sears shopping bag, a double bag. He explained, "I snagged these for free behind Sears, in the dumpster, the day after they closed the doors for good. A lot of people got some pretty good stuff that day from the dumpster. One guy got a couch, believe it or not, and somebody else got a real leather coat. Me, I just got a bunch of plastic bags. In my mind, being homeless and all, a good plastic bag trumps cowhide every time. Anyway, please take the bag and the paper inside. Open it."

I took the offered bag and opened it. Gerald was watching my face and he laughed.

"Gary, you old devil, you kept it all! How much?" I asked.

"There are ten thousand, three hundred, and seventy-five five-dollar bills — one five-dollar bill for each time you visited. Well, almost every time. I'm not a perfect man; sometimes when I was skint I would use one. Please give it to my friends when they need it and donate some to the places that helped me now and then. Buy yourself a Swiss Chalet dinner, because they helped me out from time to time with free half-chicken specials with fries."

At the hospice he put his other parcel on the ground next to his battered suitcase. Gerald stared at the hospice for a long time and made me promise not to visit him in the death place. Then he took my hand and kissed me on the cheek. "Thank you, my very dear friend the history teacher — now principal," he said. Next, he removed the steel helmet and handed it to me. "Please use this if needed. There are a lot of evil waves coming from the south."

Gerald touched the two blue stripes on his uniform and told me that he would keep the clothing and the stripes and die proudly wearing them, as so many others had done before. Finally, he picked up the parcel and handed it to me. "Open this when I have gone — gone to find my American and my friend MacDonald and his wife, the cutter of Nazi testicles. Open the thing I have given you when I am home, and think of me now and again standing by his office desk as I watch my American strut into that horrible place. Goodbye, and thank you for writing my story."

Gary walked towards the entrance but stopped just inside the death-house gate, as if deciding something of great importance. My great friend returned to where I was standing next to my car and said, "Here are a few more pages for the story. I beg that you do not think poorly of me after you read them." With that he left.

I read the pages on the spot. He died the next day, right at noon. I am told that he seemed to be holding an invisible violin, and he was smiling.

After the celebration under the overpass, I drove home with my wife in my antique Ford Mustang with the top down. We ate a takeout dinner from Swiss Chalet that Gary had paid for, and after the dishes were washed and put away, we went to the living room, as we do most nights. We opened a new bottle of single malt, toasted my friend, and stared at the package for a long time.

My wife examined the dirty paper wrapping and then handed it to me. I quickly removed the outer layer to find something encased in more Sears bags and then bubble wrap. I wept for my friend as I removed the bubbles to reveal a leather violin case.

"Oh my god," I said. "It's his violin — the old, scratched and tarnished thing that was a gift from the Nazi prison commander, that played so beautifully."

"Open the case," my wife said, knowing that I wanted to touch it, to play it.

The case was ancient, and when I held the instrument, I knew that it was old as well. I placed the Stradivarius under my chin and played the song he yearned to play for his American.

Hallelujah.

The end.
W. N.

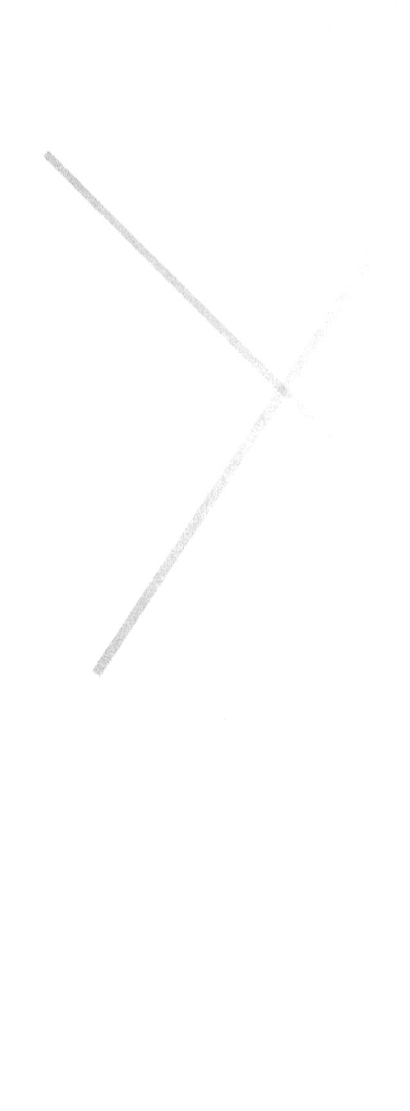